D1526393

DEEPHAVEN

Sarah Orne Jewett at her desk in her "dear old house and home."

DEEPHAVEN

BY SARAH ORNE JEWETT

ILLUSTRATED BY
CHARLES WOODBURY
AND MARCIA OAKES WOODBURY

PUBLISHED FOR THE
OLD BERWICK HISTORICAL SOCIETY
BY PETER E. RANDALL PUBLISHER
PORTSMOUTH
1993

Printed in the United States of America
Produced for the Society by
PETER E. RANDALL PUBLISHER
Box 4726, Portsmouth, New Hampshire 03801

THE OLD BERWICK HISTORICAL SOCIETY
Box 296, South Berwick, Maine 03908

The cover motif of flower vines in gold, which originally appeared on the 1893 edition of *Deephaven,* was drawn by Sarah Wyman Whitman (1842–1904), an accomplished designer of decorated trade bindings for Houghton Mifflin and the Merrymount Press. In addition to adorning Jewett's work, Whitman's graphics appeared on volumes of Thomas Bailey Aldrich, Robert Browning, Nathaniel Hawthorne, Oliver Wendell Holmes, William Dean Howells, Tacitus, Celia Thaxter, Henry Wadsworth Longfellow, John Greenleaf Whittier and Kate Douglas Wiggin. Her home on Beacon Hill, a gathering place for the literary and artistic of Boston, became in this century the home of the Club of Odd Volumes and the Society of Printers.

Library of Congress Cataloging-in-Publication Data

Jewett, Sarah Orne, 1849-1909
Deephaven / by Sarah Orne Jewett ; illustrated by Charles Woodbury and Marcia Oakes Woodbury.
p. cm.
ISBN 0-9636111-0-0
1. Seaside resorts--Maine--Fiction. 2. Young women--Maine--Fiction. I. Woodbury, Charles H. (Charles Herbert), 1864-1940. II. Woodbury, Marcia Oakes, 1865-1914. III Title.
PS2132.D4 1993
813' .4--dc20

93-3790

Introduction

When James R. Osgood & Company of Boston published *Deephaven* in the spring of 1877, Osgood sent Sarah Orne Jewett the first copy. Miss Jewett immediately wrote him to express her thanks and delight. "I think *Deephaven* is very pretty—a great deal prettier than I thought it was going to be! Don't *you* like it? I like especially the little 'die' on the back which I had not seen before." Designed in Little Classic style with covers of copper-colored cloth ornamented with a triad of cattails on the front and spine, it is indeed a pretty little book and, as the very first copy of her very first book, became especially dear to Miss Jewett. On the flyleaf she wrote: "This is the first copy of *Deephaven* that was printed and it is my own. I don't wish to lend it—there's another which can be lent in the book rack on my table. Sarah O. Jewett, April 1877."

The book sold well and brought letters of praise and appreciation from readers and reviewers, as well as requests from publishers for more manuscripts. John Greenleaf Whittier wrote that he had given several copies to friends and had just been reading it over for the third time. John Burroughs observed, "Now I know you are from Maine I can taste the flavor of the birch in your book." And from William Dean Howells, the editor of the *Atlantic Monthly* who had accepted "Mr. Bruce," the first of many Jewett stories to appear in that magazine, came this request: "Don't be too proud, now your book has succeeded so splendidly, to send some stories and sketches to your old friend, the *Atlantic Monthly*."

Reveling in the acclaim she was receiving, Miss Jewett also appreciated the royalties *Deephaven* was earning. She wrote to Osgood in September, "Is *Deephaven* still getting on well? And have you any idea how many more have been sold? I have proud thoughts of buying myself a most gallant new horse for riding." She soon had Sheila, a chestnut-colored mare, that she rode afternoons after finishing her writing.

But Miss Jewett could scarcely have foreseen that *Deephaven* would run into several editions, culminating in the handsome gift volume that appeared in November 1893. Illustrated by artists Charles Herbert and Marcia Oakes Woodbury, it was published in a large paper edition (250 numbered copies) and in a smaller format, both with white cloth spines and green cloth backs with gilt lettering and

Marcia Oakes Woodbury. "She captured on paper and canvas the essence of her own New England people."—David Oakes Woodbury. Photograph courtesy of Ruth Ruyl Woodbury.

decoration. How happy she would be to know that on its Centennial, the Old Berwick Historical Society is proudly reprinting this now rare edition.

When Sarah Jewett began to write her sketches of country and shore life in the 1870s, she remembered the lessons her father, Dr. Theodore Herman Jewett, had taught her, the things he had helped her see and understand, as they drove together to visit his patients through Old Fields and York Woods, to Heron Cove, or along what she came to call "the white rose road." In "Looking Back on Girlhood," an essay published in the *Youth's Companion* in 1892, she pointed out that he governed her first attempts at writing "by the severity and simplicity of his own good taste." "Don't try to write *about* people and things," he advised; "tell them just as they are!" It was the first and best advice Miss Jewett ever received. She had only to recall the weather-beaten farmhouses, the pebble beaches, the juniper pastures, Mrs. Snow and Aunt Polly, to portray her part of Maine authentically.

As she grew older, Miss Jewett often took solitary rambles or rides. When she rowed down the Newichawannock River, she enjoyed the company of a muskrat, gathered deckloads of cardinal flowers, watched the gulls wheel and a fishhawk plummet. In the woods and fields she explored old cellar holes and small clearings, becoming so familiar with one old farm at the edge of York Woods that she called it *her* farm, her "little kingdom." Sometimes she stopped off to visit an old farmer, crippled by wounds suffered in the Civil War; or went down Tyson's (now Vaughan's) Lane to chat with Olive Grant, the village dressmaker—"that lively, friendly, quaint, busy creature . . . My stories are full of her here and there," she wrote her friend Annie Fields.

New England was deep in a period of economic decline in the 1870s. Miss Jewett saw evidence of this decline everywhere. When she walked or rode through the outlying sections of South Berwick, she came upon forsaken farmhouses, pasture land fast reverting to woodland, stone walls that had served as boundaries tumbling down. When she rowed down the river or walked along its banks, she saw wharves rotting and crumbling and warehouses decaying.

There were several causes for the changed character and the dwindling population of New England coastal and river towns like South

Charles Herbert Woodbury from the portrait by John Singer Sargent. "In 1920 his friend John Singer Sargent and he sat for their portraits, each painting the other simultaneously." —David Oakes Woodbury. Photo courtesy of Ruth Ruyl Woodbury.

Berwick. New England shipping had never recovered from the effects of the Embargo Act of 1807 and the British blockade during the War of 1812. The coming of the railroad into northern New England in the 1840s had doomed coastal shipping, for it was soon easier and more economical to transport people and freight by rail than by sea. The gradual depletion of the forests considerably curtailed shipbuilding and the trading of lumber, once the principal business of towns like South Berwick. The Civil War had left its mark, not only claiming the lives of thousands of New England farm boys and sailors but also acquainting many New Englanders with the South and West, an acquaintance that persuaded many of them to try their luck at making a living under what seemed to them vastly easier conditions. Tiny South Berwick had sent over 200 men off to the war. Immigrants soon replaced those who had left for the South and West. They came into the little towns to work in the woolen and cotton mills that had sprung up throughout New England.

Miss Jewett was pained and disturbed by the contrast between the New England of her own day and the New England of her grandfather. In her early writing, she particularly lamented the passing of the era of the shipbuilder and merchantman and the encroachment of manufacturing on the little farming towns. Her grandfather had been part owner of four ships built in the South Berwick shipyard, ships whose names had been familiar to her from childhood. Such ships had made Berwick men familiar with Canton, Bombay, the West Indies, and London and had enabled them to bring back to Berwick a knowledge of the rest of the world. "A harbor," Miss Jewett wrote in *River Driftwood*, "even if it is a little harbor, is a good thing, since adventurers come into it as well as go out, and the life in it grows strong, because it takes something from the world, and has something to give in return." But South Berwick in the 1870s was only a station on the Boston and Maine Railroad, so insignificant that only a few trains took the trouble to stop each day. And the river was no longer a public highway but provided power for the factories, mills, and tanneries that had sprung up along its banks. Only two gundalows, flat-bottomed boats with triangular collapsible sails, sailed from the Landing wharves where forty years before at least twenty a day had put out.

Though Miss Jewett honestly admitted that "it was impossible to estimate the value of that wider life that was flowing in from the great springs," she could not help being apprehensive about many of these changes. Nevertheless, she set herself the task of interpreting her part of Maine in this period of transition with a series of sketches. The first of these, "The Shore House," was enthusiastically accepted in 1873 by the *Atlantic Monthly*, whose editor, William Dean Howells, begged her to write more pieces of the same kind. She complied with "Deephaven Cronies" and "Deephaven Excursions." They were so well received that Howells suggested she combine the sketches in a book. Connecting them involved inventing a framework or structure and doing some rearranging. To unite the sketches, she used a summer visitor to Deephaven as the narrator, a device she used much more successfully some twenty years later in *The Country of the Pointed Firs*, her masterpiece.

The Brandon house that the summer visitor stays in with her friend resembles very closely Miss Jewett's own home, and Deephaven itself, though she always maintained that it "was not to be found on the map of New England under another name, and that the characters were seldom drawn from life," was unmistakably a composite of Kittery, York, Ogunquit, and Wells, shore towns with which Miss Jewett was almost as familiar and loved quite as much as her native South Berwick. The narrator and her friend walk along Long and Short Sands, visit Spouting Rock and Bald Head Cliff, row out to Deephaven Light, so like the lighthouse at the Nubble in York. The old seamen, Captains Sands and Captain Lant, who might be seen "every pleasant morning sunning themselves like turtles on one of the wharves," resemble the retired captains Miss Jewett frequently visited in Wells and York in the old fish houses along the wharves. She brought them books occasionally, one of them asking for "some good books of stories, *detective ones*, none of your lovesick kind," which he couldn't go! The prototypes of Mrs. Kew, the wise, hardworking wife of the island lighthouse keeper; the "Widow Jim" Patton, that useful character who could do everything from turning a carpet to brewing countless varieties of herb tea; the entertaining, unconventional Mrs. Bonny, who lived alone on the side of the mountain (Agamenticus, no doubt) and who knew intimately all the herbs and trees and wild animals; the elderly bachelor "Mr. Dick" Carew, formerly a merchant in the East Indies, who now spent most of his time in his library getting fuel for his arguments with the minister, the Reverend Mr. Lorimer; the sunburnt, weatherbeaten Danny, silent and lame, who like so many Deephaven men who had shipped before the mast in their youth, now trawled for mackerel or pulled his lobster traps each morning; all of these had their counterparts in Miss Jewett's native or neighboring towns. My Lady Brandon of Deephaven could well have been the actual Miss Cushing of South Berwick, the grand old lady whom Miss Jewett dearly loved to visit in her childhood and for whom she always put on her best manners and behavior. General Lafayette had paid a ceremonious call on Miss Cushing's mother during his triumphant tour of America in 1825, an honor of which South Berwick was as proud as were the people of Deephaven of the fact that their little town had once been the residence of one Governor Chantrey. And Miss Chauncey, Miss Jewett wrote to a friend, was Miss Sally Chauncey Cutts, whom she had visited one afternoon in the Lady Pepperrell house at Kittery Point. "Very little of that chapter is imaginary (or of the chapter called 'In Shadow')."

And the speech of her village and shore people. Even this first of her books reveals how closely she observed and recorded it. From childhood she had treasured the terse, pungent talk she heard on the wharves and in the farmhouse kitchens though she apparently was not aware of watching or listening. Listen to old Mrs. Dockum speaking of one of her neighbors: "Willin' woman, always been respected; got an uncommon facility o' speech. I never saw such a hand to talk, but then she has something to say, which ain't the case with everybody." Or one of the old fishermen, Danny, describing a mackerel: "Not to say but I've seen more fancy-looking fish down in southern waters, bright as any flower you ever see; but a mackerel, why they're so clean-built and trig-looking! Put a cod alongside, and he looks as lumbering as an old-fashioned Dutch brig aside a yacht." Anyone conversing with an old inhabitant of a small Maine town today hears the same talk. Miss Jewett caught the distinctive flavor of farm and shore speech—the occasional use of an unexpected word, the ungrammatical but picturesque phrase, the colorful comparisons, the inflections, the very rhythm of Maine dialect.

When the continuing popularity of *Deephaven* persuaded the publishers to issue the 1893 gift edition, they chose Charles Herbert and Marcia Oakes Woodbury to do the illustrations. The choice of artists was undoubtedly at the request of Miss Jewett. She and Susan Marcia Oakes Woodbury were old friends and had much in common. Both were South Berwick natives, Sarah the daughter of the beloved country doctor, Theodore H. Jewett, and Susan Marcia the daughter of the highly respected village lawyer and probate judge, Abner C. Oakes. Both were graduates of Berwick Academy, Maine's oldest academy, which their fathers served as trustees for many years, Judge Oakes as secretary and treasurer, and where Susy, as she was called as a girl, taught classes in art. And both were exceptionally gifted and determined to pursue their chosen careers.

Marcia Oakes studied art under Charles Woodbury, first at his school in Swampscott, Massachusetts, then in Boston, and fell in love not only with painting but with her teacher. Some years after their marriage they came to live in Ogunquit where Charles Woodbury established the first summer school of art. A native of Lynn, he knew and loved the New England coast and countryside as his wife and Sarah Jewett did—had painted the sea in all its moods off Swampscott, Beverly, and Gloucester before he came to Maine. An honors graduate of Massachusetts Institute of Technology with a degree in mechanical engineering, he studied at the Boston Art Club and the Academie Julian and as both engineer and artist was fascinated with the ever changing, shifting surfaces of the sea.

Proof of the authenticity of Miss Jewett's portrayal of Deephaven and its people is evident in the Woodburys' illustrations. Most of the portraits were drawn of real people. The Widow Tully is Marcia Oakes Woodbury's mother; Mrs. Patton (the Widow Jim) is Charles Woodbury's mother. Mr. Dick and Mr. Lorimer are Reverend David B. Sewall, pastor of the Congregational Church in South Berwick, and Judge Oakes. Miss Rebecca Lorimer in "The Sunday Dinner" is Mrs. David Sewall. The frontispiece, "The Brandon House," is the Colonel Jonathan Hamilton house though the fence in front of it is modeled on that of the Judge William Allen Hayes house on Academy Street, South Berwick. The interiors of the Brandon house—the spacious center hall, the library where Mr. Dick and

Parson Lorimer argued over certain points of theology, the dining room, the parlor where Miss Brandon had played the piano in the twilight—all depict Sarah Jewett's own home. Indeed, Babette Ann Boleman in an article published in *The Colophon* in August 1939 explained that Miss Jewett marked a copy of the book with suggestions for subjects for the Woodburys, most of which they apparently followed.

In her beautiful preface to this 1893 edition of *Deephaven* Miss Jewett wrote: "There is a noble saying of Plato that the best thing that can be done for the people of a state is to make them acquainted with one another." With her first book she did just that. She succeeded in portraying the everyday life of the New England small town of her youth and in interpreting her country and shore people to her readers. Nothing much happens in *Deephaven*, but then nothing much happened in the lives of these people. It was a prosaic, humdrum existence that they led, and Miss Jewett would have been dishonest had she tried to picture it otherwise.

Though she knew the book had its faults—the rather weak narrative structure, the technical unevenness, "the sentences which make her feel as if she were the grandmother of the author of *Deephaven*"—she had a special fondness for this first of her many books. Speaking of *Deephaven* and *The Tory Lover*, her last book, in a letter to William Dean Howells not many years before her death, she wrote: "But the two together hold all my knowledge, real knowledge, and all my dreams about my dear Berwick and York and Wells—the people I know and have heard about: the very dust of thought and association that made me!"

South Berwick
February 1993

Marie Donahue

The Marcia Oakes Woodbury Sketchbook

When planning her *Deephaven* illustrations in 1893, and living with her husband at her parents' South Berwick home a short walk from the door of Sarah Orne Jewett, artist Marcia Oakes Woodbury made use of a white clothbound four-by-seven-inch sketchbook.

In addition to trying rough studies of many scenes from the novel, the artist also planned her *Deephaven* work in pencilled notes, month by month from April through July of that year, and subject by subject, from "Captain Sands (Uncle Gray)" to "Miss Chauncey (Auntie)"—probably references to two Woodbury relatives who would serve as models for Jewett's characters.

A century later, in 1990, volunteers found Woodbury's sketchbook among some undocumented artifacts of the Old Berwick Historical Society, a brick building a few streets from where she had worked. Together its pages show some of the care with which the artist drew her creations from the simple faces and gestures of southern Maine folk.

Circus study
Final drawing page 161

Mrs. Bonny studies
Final drawing page 239

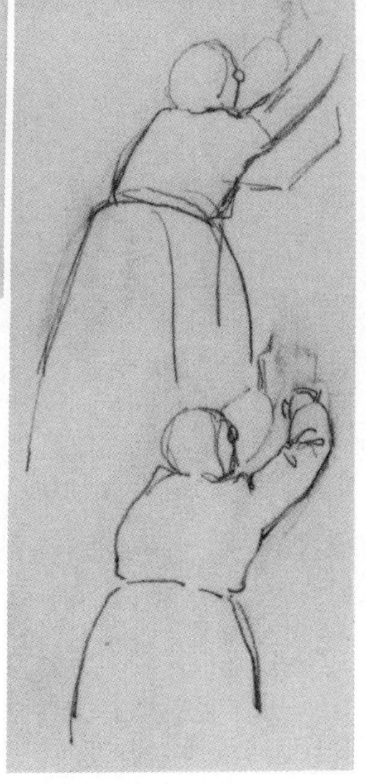

One Young Girl studies
Final drawing page 31

The Brandon House

DEEPHAVEN

BY SARAH ORNE JEWETT

ILLUSTRATED BY
CHARLES AND MARCIA
WOODBURY

BOSTON AND NEW YORK
HOUGHTON, MIFFLIN AND COMPANY
The Riverside Press, Cambridge
M DCCC XCIV

The Riverside Press, Cambridge, Mass., U. S. A.
Electrotyped and Printed by H. O. Houghton & Co.

Contents and List of Illustrations

From Designs by

Charles Herbert and Marcia Oakes Woodbury

Preface

The short lifetime of this little book has seen great changes in the conditions of provincial life in New England. Twenty years ago, or a little more, the two heroines whose simple adventures are here described might well have served as types of those pioneers who were already on the eager quest for rural pleasures. Twenty years ago, our fast-growing New England cities, which had so lately been but large towns, full of green gardens and quiet neighborhoods, were just beginning to be overcrowded and uncomfortable in summer. The steady inflow of immigration, and the way in which these cities had drawn to themselves, like masses of quicksilver, much of the best life of the remotest villages, had made necessary a reflex current that set countryward in summer. This presently showed itself to be of unsuspected force and significance: it meant something more than the instinct for green fields and hills and the sea-shore; crowded towns and the open country were to be brought together in new association and dependence upon each other. It appeared as if a second Harvey had discovered a new and national circulation of vitality along the fast-multiplying railroads that spun their webs to bind together men who had once lived far apart. The civil war, which had given so many citizens of the North their first journey and first knowledge of the world outside their native parishes; the fashion set before the war by those gay Southerners who for the most part filled the few mountain and sea-shore hotels of the North; the increase of wealth, and of the number of persons who had houses in town and country both, — all these causes brought about great and almost sudden changes in rustic life. Old farmhouses opened their doors to the cheerful gayety of summer; the old jokes about the respective aggressions and ignorances of city and country cousins gave place to new compliments between the summer boarder and his rustic host. It began to appear that neither men nor women of the great towns were any longer stayers-at-home according to the Scripture admonition.

The young writer of these Deephaven sketches was possessed by a dark fear that townspeople and country people would never understand one another, or learn to profit by their new relationship. She may have had the unconscious desire to make some sort of explanation to those who still expected to find the caricatured Yankee of fiction, striped trousers, bell-crowned hat, and all, driving his steady horses along the shady roads. It seemed not altogether reasonable when timid ladies mistook a selectman for a tramp, because he happened to be crossing a field in his shirt sleeves. At the same time, she was sensible of grave wrong and misunderstanding when these same timid ladies were regarded with suspicion, and their kindnesses were believed to come from pride and patronage. There is a noble saying of Plato that the best thing that can be done for the people of a state is to make them acquainted with one another. It was, happily, in the writer's childhood that Mrs. Stowe had written of those who dwelt along the wooded seacoast and by the decaying, shipless harbors of Maine. The first chapters of "The Pearl of Orr's Island" gave the young author of "Deephaven" to see with new eyes, and to follow eagerly the old shore paths from one gray, weather-beaten house to another where Genius pointed her the way.

In those days, if one had just passed her twentieth year, it was easy to be much disturbed by the sad discovery that certain phases of provincial life were fast waning in New England. Small and old-fashioned towns, of which Deephaven may, by the reader's courtesy, stand as a type, were no longer almost self-subsistent, as in earlier times; and while it was impossible to estimate the value of that wider life that was flowing in from the great springs, many a mournful villager felt the anxiety that came with these years of change. Tradition and time-honored custom were to be swept away together by the irresistible current. Character and architecture seemed to lose individuality and distinction. The new riches of the country were seldom very well spent in those days; the money that the tourist or summer citizen left behind him was apt to be used to sweep away the quaint houses, the roadside thicket, the shady woodland, that had lured him first; and the well-filled purses that were scattered in our country's first great triumphal impulse of prosperity often came into the hands of people who hastened to spoil instead of to mend the best things that their village held. It will remain for later generations to make amends for the sad use of riches after the war, for our injury of what we inherited, for the irreparable loss of certain ancient buildings which would have been twice as interesting in the next century as we are just beginning to be wise enough to think them in this.

That all the individuality and quaint personal characteristics of rural New England were so easily swept away, or are even now dying out, we can refuse to believe. It appears, even, that they are better nourished and shine brighter by contrast than in former years. In rustic neighborhoods there will always be those whom George Sand had in mind when she wrote her delightful preface for "Légendes Rustiques:" "Le paysan est donc, si l'on peut ainsi dire, le seul historien qui nous reste des temps antehistorique. Honneur et profit intellectuel à qui se consacrerait à la recherche de ses traditions merveilleuses de chaque hameau qui rassemblées ou groupées, comparées entre elles et minutieusement disséquées, jetteraient peut-être de grandes lueurs sur la nuit profonde des âges primitifs." There will also exist that other class of country people who preserve the best traditions of culture and of manners, from some divine inborn instinct toward what is simplest and best and purest, who know the best because they themselves are of kin to it. It is as hard to be just to our contemporaries as it is easy to borrow enchantment in looking at the figures of the past; but while the Judges and Governors and grand ladies of old Deephaven are being lamented, we must not forget to observe that it is Miss Carew and Miss Lorimer who lament them, and who insist that there are no representatives of the ancient charm and dignity of their beloved town. Human nature is the same the world over, provincial and rustic influences must ever produce much the same effects upon character, and town life will ever have in its gift the spirit of the present, while it may take again from the quiet of hills and fields and the conservatism of country hearts a gift from the spirit of the past.

In the Preface to the first edition of "Deephaven" it was explained that Deephaven was not to be found on the map of New England under another name, and that the characters were seldom drawn from life. It was often asserted to the contrary, while the separate chapters were being published from time to time in "The Atlantic Monthly," and made certain where the town really was, and the true names of its citizens and pew-holders. Therefore it appeared there were already many "places in America," not "few," that were "touched with the hue of decay." Portsmouth and York and Wells, which were known to the author, Fairhaven and other seacoast towns, which were unknown, were spoken of as the originals of this fictitious village which still exists only in the mind. Strangely enough, the Atlantic Ocean always seems to lie to the west of it rather than to the east, and the landscape generally takes its own way and furnishes impossible landmarks and impressions to the one person who can see it clearly and in large. Some early knowledge of the secret found later in the delightful story of "Peter Ibbetson" appears to have been foreseen, but a lack of experience and a limited knowledge of the wide world outside forced the imaginer of Deephaven to build her dear town of such restricted materials as lay within her grasp. The landscape itself is always familiar to her thought, and far more real than many others which have been seen since with preoccupied or tired eyes.

The writer frankly confesses that the greater part of any value which these sketches may possess is in their youthfulness. There are sentences which make her feel as if she were the grandmother of the author of "Deephaven" and her heroines, those "two young ladies of virtue and honour, bearing an inviolable friendship for each other," as two others, less fortunate, are described in the preface to "Clarissa Harlowe." She begs her readers to smile with her over those sentences as they are found not seldom along the pages, and so the callow wings of what thought itself to be wisdom and the childish soul of sentiment will still be happy and untroubled.

In a curious personal sense the author repeats her attempt to explain the past and the present to each other. This little book will remind some of those friends who read it first of

> *"—light that lit the olden days;"*

but there are kind eyes, unknown then, that are very dear now, and to these the pages will be new. This Preface must end as the first Preface ended, with a dedication to my father and mother—my two best friends—and then to all my other friends whose names I say to myself lovingly, though I do not write them here.

S. O. J.

SOUTH BERWICK, MAINE, *October*, 1893.

Kate Lancaster's Plan

I HAD been spending the winter in Boston, and Kate Lancaster and I had been together a great deal, for we are the best of friends. It happened that the morning when this story begins I had waked up feeling sorry, and as if something dreadful were going to happen. There did not seem to be any good reason for it, so I undertook to discourage myself more by thinking that it would soon be time to leave town, and how much I should miss being with Kate and my other friends. My mind was still disquieted when I went down to breakfast; but beside my plate I found, with a hoped-for letter from my father, who was in China, a note from Kate. To this day I have never known any explanation of that depression of my spirits, and I hope that the good luck which followed will help some reader to lose fear, and to smile at such shadows if any chance to come.

Kate had evidently written to me in an excited state of mind, for her note was not so trig-looking as usual; but this is what she said: —

DEAR HELEN, — I have a plan — I think it a most delightful plan — in which you and I are chief characters. Promise that you will say yes; if you do not, you will have to remember all your life that you broke a girl's heart. Come round early, and lunch with me and dine with me. I 'm to be all alone, and it 's a long story and will need a great deal of talking over.

K.

I showed this note to my aunt, and soon went round, very much interested. My latch-key opened the Lancasters' door, and I hurried to the parlor, where I heard my friend practicing with great diligence. I went up to her, and she turned her head and kissed me solemnly. You need not smile; we are not sentimental girls, and are both much averse to indiscriminate kissing, though I have not the adroit habit of shying in which Kate is proficient. It would sometimes be impolite in any one else, but she shies so affectionately.

"Won't you sit down, dear?" she said, with great ceremony, and went on with her playing, which was abominable that morning; her fingers stepped on each other, and, whatever the tune might have been in reality, it certainly had a most remarkable incoherence as I heard it then. I took up the new Littell and made believe read it, and finally threw it at Kate; you would have thought we were two children.

"Have you heard that my grand-aunt, Miss Katharine Brandon of Deephaven, is dead?"

I knew that she had died in November, at least six months before. "Don't be nonsensical, Kate!" said I. "What do you mean to tell me?"

"My grand-aunt died very old, and was the last of her generation. She had a sister and three brothers, one of whom had the honor of being my grandfather. Mamma is sole heir to the family estates in Deephaven, wharf-property and all, and it is a great inconvenience to her. The house is a charming old house, and some of my ancestors who followed the sea brought home the greater part of its furnishings. Miss Katharine was a person who ignored all frivolities, and her house was as sedate as herself. I have been there but little, for when I was a child my aunt found no pleasure in the society of noisy children who upset her treasures, and when I was older she did not care to see strangers, and after I left school she grew more and more feeble; I had not been there for two years when she died. Mamma went down very often. The town is a quaint old place which has seen better days. There are high rocks at the shore, and there is a beach, and there are woods inland, and hills, and there is the sea. It might be dull in Deephaven for two young ladies who were fond of gay society and depended upon excitement, I suppose; but for two little girls who were fond of each other and could play in the boats, and dig and build houses in the sea-sand, and gather shells, and carry their dolls wherever they went, what could be pleasanter?"

"Nothing," said I promptly.

Kate had told this a little at a time, with a few appropriate bars of music between, which suddenly reminded me of the story of a Chinese procession which I had read in one of Marryat's novels when I was a child: "A thousand white elephants richly caparisoned,

—ti-tum tilly-lily," and so on, for a page or two. She seemed to have finished her story for that time, and while it was dawning upon me what she meant, she sang a bit from one of Jean Ingelow's verses: —

> "Will ye step aboard, my dearest,
> For the high seas lie before us?"

and then came over to sit beside me and tell the whole story in a more sensible fashion.

"You know that my father has been meaning to go to England in the autumn? Yesterday he told us that he is to leave in a month and will be away all summer, and mamma is going with him. Jack and Willy are to join a party of their classmates who are to spend nearly the whole of the long vacation at Lake Superior. I don't wish to go abroad again now, and I did not like any plan that was proposed to me. Aunt Anna was here all the afternoon, and is willing to take the house at Newport, which is very pleasant and unexpected, for she hates housekeeping. Mamma thought of course that I should stay with her, but I did not wish to do that, and it would only result in my keeping house for her visitors, whom I know very little; and she will be much more free and independent by herself. Beside, she can have my room if I am not there. I have promised to make her a long visit in Baltimore next winter instead. I told mamma that I should like to stay here and go away when I choose. There are ever so many visits which I have promised; I could stay with you and your Aunt Mary at Lenox if she goes there, for a while, and I have always wished to spend a whole summer in town; but mamma did not encourage that at all. In the evening papa gave her a letter which had come from Mr. Dockum, the man who takes care of Aunt Katharine's place, and the most charming idea came into my head, and I said that I meant to spend my summer in Deephaven.

"At first they laughed at me, and then they said I might go if I chose, and at last they thought nothing could be pleasanter, and mamma wishes now that she were going herself. I asked if she did not think you would be the best person to keep me company, and she does, and papa announced that he was just going to suggest my asking you. I am to take Ann and Maggie, who will be overjoyed, for they came from that part of the country, and the other servants are to go with Aunt Anna, and old Nora will come to take care of this house, as she always does. Perhaps you and I will come up to town once in a while for a few days. We shall have such jolly housekeeping. Mamma and I sat up very late last night, and everything is planned. Mr. Dockum's house is very near Aunt Katharine's, so we shall not be lonely; though I know you 're no more afraid of that than I. O Helen, won't you go?"

Do you think it took me long to decide?

Mr. and Mrs. Lancaster sailed the 10th of June, and my Aunt Mary went to spend her summer among the Berkshire Hills, so I was at the Lancasters' ready to welcome Kate when she came home, after having said good-by to her father and mother. We meant to go to Deephaven in a week, but were obliged to stay in town longer. Boston was nearly deserted of our friends at the last, and we used to take quiet walks in the cool of the evening after dinner, up and down the street, or sit on the front steps in company with the people left in charge of the other houses, who also sometimes walked up and down and looked at us wonderingly. We had much shopping to do in the daytime, for there was a probability of our spending many days indoors, and as we were not to be near any large town, and did not mean to come to Boston for weeks at least, there was a great deal to be remembered and arranged. We enjoyed making our plans, and deciding what we should want, and going to the shops together. I think we felt most important the day we conferred with Ann and made out a list of the provisions which must be ordered. This was being house-keepers in earnest. Mr. Dockum happened

The Stage-Coach

to come to town, and we sent Ann and Maggie, with most of our boxes, to Deephaven in his company a day or two before we were ready to go ourselves, and when we reached there the house was opened and in order for us.

On our journey to Deephaven we left the railway twelve miles from that place, and took passage in a stage-coach. There was only one passenger beside ourselves. She was a very large, thin, weather-beaten woman, and looked so tired and lonesome and good-natured, that I could not help saying it was very dusty; and she was apparently delighted to answer that she should think everybody was sweeping, and she always felt, after being in the cars awhile, as if she had been taken all to pieces and left in the different places. This was the beginning of our friendship with Mrs. Kew.

After this conversation we looked industriously out of the window into the pastures and pine woods. I had given up my seat to her, for I do not mind riding backward in the least, and you would have thought I had done her the greatest favor of her life. I think she was the most grateful of women, and I was often reminded of a remark one of my friends once made about some one: "If you give Bessie a half-sheet of letter paper, she behaves to you as if it were the most exquisite of presents!" Kate and I had some fruit left in our lunch basket, and divided it with Mrs. Kew, but after the first mouthful we looked at each other in dismay. "Lemons with oranges' clothes on, aren't they?" said she, as Kate threw hers out of the window, and mine went after it for company; and after this we began to be very friendly indeed. We both liked the odd woman, there was something so straightforward and kindly about her.

"Are you going to Deephaven, dear?" she asked me, and then: "I wonder if you are going to stay long? All summer? Well, that 's clever! I do hope you will come out to the Light to see me; young folks 'most always like my place. Most likely your friends will fetch you."

"Do you know the Brandon house?" asked Kate.

"Well as I do the meeting-house. There! I wonder I did n't know from the beginning, but I had been a-trying all the way to settle it who you could be. I 've been up country some weeks, stopping with my mother, and she seemed so set to have me stay till strawberry-time and would hardly let me come now. You see, she 's getting to be old; why, every time I 've come away for fifteen years she 's said it was the last time I 'd ever see her, but she 's a dreadful smart woman of her age. 'He' wrote me some o' Mrs. Lancaster's folks were going to take the Brandon house this summer; and so you are the ones? It 's a sightly old place; I used to go and see Miss Katharine. She must have left a power of china-ware. She set a great deal by the house, and she kept everything just as it used to be in her mother's day."

"Then you live in Deephaven too?" asked Kate.

"I 've been here the better part of my life. I was raised up among the hills in Vermont, and I shall always be a real up-country woman if I live here a hundred years. The sea does n't come natural to me, it kind of worries me, though you won't find a happier woman than I be, 'long shore. When I was first married 'he' had a schooner and went to the Banks, and once he was off on a whaling voyage, and I hope I may never come to so long a three years as those were again, though I was up to mother's. Before I was married he had been 'most everywhere. When he came home that time from whaling, he found I 'd taken it so to heart that he said he 'd never go off again, and then he got the chance to keep Deephaven Light, and we 've lived there seventeen years come January. There is n't no great pay, but then nobody tries to get it away from us, and we 've got so 's to be contented, if it is lonesome in winter."

"Do you really live in the lighthouse? I remember how I used to beg to be taken out there when I was a child, and how I used to watch for the light at night," said Kate, enthusiastically.

So began a friendship which we both still treasure, for knowing Mrs. Kew was one of the pleasantest things which happened to us in that delightful summer, and she used to do so much for our pleasure, and was so good to us. When we went out to the lighthouse for the last time to say good-by, we were very sorry girls indeed. We had no idea until then how much she cared for us, and her affection touched us very much. She told us that she loved us as if we belonged to her, and begged us not to forget her, — as if we ever could! — and to remember that there was always a home and a warm heart for us if she were alive. Kate and I have often agreed that few of our acquaintances are half so entertaining. Her comparisons were most striking and amusing, and her comments upon the books she read — for she was a great reader — were very shrewd and clever, and always to the point. She was never out of temper, even when the barrels of oil were being rolled across her kitchen floor. And she was such a wise woman! This stage-ride, which we expected to find tiresome, we enjoyed very much, and we were glad

Mrs. Kew

to think, when the coach stopped, and "he" came to meet her with great satisfaction, that we had one friend in Deephaven at all events.

I liked the house from my very first sight of it. It stood behind a row of poplars which were as green and flourishing as the poplars which stand in stately processions in the fields around Quebec. It was an imposing great white house, and the lilacs were tall, and there were crowds of rosebushes not yet out of bloom; and there were box borders, and there were great elms at the side of the house and down the road. The hall door stood wide open, and my hostess turned to me as we went in, with one of her sweet, sudden smiles. "Won't we have a good time, Nelly?" said she. And I thought we should.

So our summer's housekeeping began in most pleasant fashion. It was just at sunset, and Ann's and Maggie's presence made the house seem familiar at once. Maggie had been unpacking for us, and there was a delicious supper for the hungry girls. Later in the evening we went down to the shore, which was not very far away; the fresh sea-air was welcome after the dusty day, and it seemed so quiet and pleasant in Deephaven.

The Brandon House and the Lighthouse

I DO not know that the Brandon house is really very remarkable, but I never have been in one that interested me in the same way. Kate used to recount to select audiences at school some of her experiences with her Aunt Katharine, and it was popularly believed that she once carried down some indestructible picture-books when they were first in fashion, and the old lady basted them for her to hem round the edges at the rate of two a day. It may have been fabulous. It was impossible to imagine any children in the old place; everything was for grown people; even the stair-railing was too high to slide down on. The chairs looked as if they had been put, at the furnishing of the house, in their places, and there they meant to remain. The carpets were particularly interesting, and I remember Kate's pointing out to me one day a great square figure in one, and telling me she used to keep house there with her dolls for lack of a better play-house, and if one of them chanced to fall outside the boundary stripe, it was immediately put to bed with a cold. It is a house with great possibilities; it might easily be made charming. There are four very large rooms on the lower floor, and six above, a wide hall in each story, and a fascinating garret over the whole, where were many mysterious old chests and boxes, in one of which we found Kate's grandmother's love-letters; and you may be sure the vista of rummages which Mr. Lancaster had laughed about was explored to its very end. The rooms all have elaborate cornices, and the lower hall is very fine, with an archway dividing it, and panelings of all sorts, and a great door at each end, through which the lilacs in front and the old pensioner plum-trees in the garden are seen exchanging bows and gestures. Coming from the Lancasters' high city house, it did not seem as if we had to go upstairs at all there, for every step of the stairway is so broad and low, and you come halfway to a square landing with an old straight-backed chair in each farther corner; and between them a large round-topped window, with a cushioned seat, looking out on the garden and the village, the hills far inland, and the sunset beyond all. Then you turn and go up a few more steps to the upper hall, where we used to stay a great deal. There were more old chairs and a pair of remarkable sofas, on which we used to deposit the treasures collected in our wanderings. The wide window which looks out on the lilacs and the sea was a favorite seat of ours. Facing each other on either side of it are two old secretaries, and one of them we ascertained to be the hiding-place of secret drawers, in which may be found valuable records deposited by ourselves one rainy day when we first explored it. We wrote, between us, a tragic "journal" on some yellow old letter-paper we found in the desk. We put it in the most hidden drawer by itself, and flatter ourselves that it will be regarded with great interest some time or other. Of one of the front rooms, "the best chamber," we stood rather in dread. It is very remarkable that there seem to be no ghost-stories connected with any part of the house, particularly this. We are neither of us nervous ; but there is certainly something dismal about the room. The huge curtained bed and immense easy-chairs, windows, and everything were draped in some old-fashioned kind of white cloth which always seemed to be waving and moving about of itself. The carpet was most singularly colored with dark reds and indescribable grays and browns, and the pattern, after a whole summer's study, could never be followed with one's eye. The paper was captured in a French prize somewhere, some time in the last century, and part of the figure was shaggy, and therein little spiders found habitation, and went visiting their acquaintances across the shiny places. The color was an unearthly pink and a forbidding maroon, with dim white spots, which gave it the appearance of having moulded. It made you low-spirited to look long in the mirror; and the great lounge one could not have cheerful associations with, after hearing that Miss Brandon herself did not like it, having seen so many of her relatives lie there dead. There were fantastic china ornaments from Bible subjects on the mantel, and the only picture was one of the Maid of Orleans tied with an unnecessarily strong rope to a very stout stake. The best parlor we also rarely used, because all the portraits which hung there had for some unaccountable reason taken a violent dislike to us, and followed us suspiciously with their eyes. The furniture was stately and very uncomfortable, and there was something about the room which suggested an invisible funeral.

There is not very much to say about the dining-room. It was not specially interesting, though the sea was in sight from the windows. There were some old Dutch pictures on the wall, so dark that one could scarcely make out what they were meant to represent, and one or two engravings. There was a huge sideboard, for which Kate had brought down from Boston Miss Brandon's own silver which had stood there for so many years, and looked so much more at home and in place than any other possibly could have looked, and Kate also found in the closet the three great decanters, with silver labels chained round their necks, which had always been companions of the tea-service in her aunt's lifetime. From the little closets in the sideboard came a most significant odor of cake and wine whenever one opened the doors. We used Miss Brandon's beautiful old blue china, which she had given to Kate, and which had been carefully packed all winter as if to be taken away. Kate sat at the head and I at the foot of the round table, and I must confess that we were apt to have either a feast or a famine, for at first we often forgot to provide our dinners. If this were the case, Maggie was sure to serve us with most derisive elegance, and make us wait for as much ceremony as she thought necessary for one of Mrs. Lancaster's dinner-parties.

The west parlor was our favorite room down-stairs. It had a great fireplace framed in blue and white Dutch tiles, which ingeniously and instructively represented the careers of the good and the bad man; the starting place of each being a very singular cradle in the centre at the top. The last two of the series are very high art; a great coffin stands in the foreground of each, and the virtuous man is being led off by two disagreeable-looking angels, while the wicked one is hastening from an indescribable but unpleasant assemblage of claws and horns and eyes which is rapidly advancing from the distance, open-mouthed, and bringing a chain with it.

There was a large cabinet holding all the small curiosities and knick-knacks there seemed to be no other place for, — odd china figures and cups and vases, unaccountable Chinese carvings and exquisite corals and sea-shells, minerals and Swiss wood-work, and articles of *vertu* from the South Seas. Underneath were stored boxes of letters and old magazines; for this was one of the houses where nothing seems to have been thrown away. In one parting we found a parcel of old manuscript sermons, the existence of which was a mystery, until Kate remembered there had been a gifted son of the house who entered the ministry and soon died. The windows of this room had each a pane of beautiful old stained glass in the upper and lower sashes, apparently taken from some older English house, with quaint shields and crests, and on the wide sills beneath we used to put our immense bouquets of field flowers. There was one place which I liked and sat in more than any other. The chimney filled nearly the whole side of the room, all but this little corner, where there was just room for a very comfortable high-backed cushioned chair, and a narrow window where I always had a bunch of fresh green ferns in a tall champagne-glass. I used to write there often, and always sat there when Kate sang and played. She sent for a tuner, and used to successfully coax the long-imprisoned music from the antiquated piano, and sing for her visitors by the hour. She almost always sang her oldest songs, for they seemed most in keeping with everything about us. I used to fancy that the portraits liked our being there. There was one young girl who seemed solitary and forlorn among the rest in the room, who were all middle-aged. For their part they looked amiable, but rather unhappy, as if she had come in, and interrupted their conversation. We both grew very fond of her, and it seemed, when we went in the last morning on purpose to take leave of her, as if she looked at us imploringly. She was soon afterward boxed up, and now enjoys society after her own heart in Kate's room in Boston.

One Young Girl

There was the largest sofa I ever saw

opposite the fireplace; it must have been brought in in pieces, and built in the room. It was broad enough for Kate and me to lie on together with our books, and was very high and square; but there was a pile of soft cushions at either end. We used to enjoy it very much in September, when the evenings were long and cool, and we had many candles, and a fire — and crickets too — on the hearth, and the dear dog lying on the rug. I remember one rainy night, just before our friends Miss Tennant and Kitty Bruce went away; we had a real driftwood fire, and blew out the lights and told stories. Kate and I were unusually entertaining, for we became familiar with the family record of the town, and could recount marvelous adventures by land and sea, and ghost-stories by the dozen. We had never either of us been in a society consisting of so many traveled people! Hardly a man but had been the most of his life at sea. Speaking of ghost-stories, I must tell you that once in the summer two Cambridge girls, who were spending a week with us, unwisely enticed us into giving some thrilling recitals, which nearly frightened them out of their wits, and Kate and I were finally in terror ourselves. We had all been on the sofa in the dark, singing and talking, and were waiting in great suspense after I had finished one of such particular horror that I declared it should be the last, when we heard footsteps on the hall stairs. There were lights in the dining-room which shone faintly through the half-closed door, and we saw something white and shapeless come slowly down, and clutched each other's gowns in agony. It was only Kate's great dog, who came in and laid his head in her lap and slept peacefully. We thought we could not sleep a wink after this, and I bravely went alone out to the light to see my watch, and, finding it was past twelve, we concluded to sit up all night and to go down to the shore at sunrise, it would be so much easier than getting up early some morning. We had been out rowing and had taken a long walk the day before, and were obliged to dance and make other slight exertions to keep ourselves awake at one time. We lunched at two, and I never shall forget the sunrise that morning; but we were singularly quiet and abstracted that day, and indeed for several days after Deephaven was "a land in which it seemed always afternoon," we breakfasted so late.

As Mrs. Kew had said, there was "a power of china." Kate and I were convinced that the lives of her grandmothers must have been spent in giving tea parties. We counted ten sets of cups, besides quantities of stray ones; and some member of the family had evidently devoted her time to making a collection of pitchers.

There was an escritoire in Miss Brandon's own room, which we looked over one day. There was a little package of letters; ship letters mostly, tied with a very pale and tired-looking blue ribbon. They were in a drawer with a locket holding a faded miniature on ivory and a lock of brown hair, and there were also some dry twigs and bits of leaf which had long ago been bright wild roses, such as still bloom among the Deephaven rocks. Kate said that she had often heard her mother wonder why her aunt never had cared to marry, for she had chances enough doubtless, and had been rich and handsome and finely educated. So there was a sailor-lover after all, and perhaps he had been lost at sea and she faithfully kept the secret, never mourning outwardly. "And I always thought her the most matter-of-fact old lady," said Kate; "yet here's her romance, after all." We put the letters outside on a chair to read, but afterwards carefully replaced them, without untying them. I 'm glad we did, but we felt more than heroic at the time. There were other letters which we did read, and which interested us very much, — letters from her girl friends written in the boarding-school vacations and just after she finished school. Those in one of the smaller packages were charming; it must have been such a bright, nice girl who wrote them! They were very few, and were tied with black ribbon, and marked on the outside in girlish writing: "My dearest friend, Dolly McAllister, died September 3, 1809, aged eighteen." The ribbon had evidently been untied and the letters read many times. One began: "My dear, delightful Kitten: I am quite overjoyed to find my father has business which will force him to go to Deephaven next week, and he kindly says if there be no more rain I may ride with him to see you. I will surely come, for if there is danger of spattering my gown and he bids me stay at home, I shall go galloping after him and overtake him when it is too late to send me back. I have so much to tell you." I wish we knew more about the visit. Poor Miss Katharine! it made us sad to look over these treasures of her girlhood. There were her compositions and exercise-books; some samplers and queer little keepsakes; withered flowers and some pretty pebbles and other things of like value, with which there was probably some pleasant association. "Only think of her keeping them all her days," said I to Kate. "I am continually throwing some relic of the kind away, because I forget why I have it!"

There was a box in the lower part which Kate was glad to find, for she had heard her mother wonder if some such things were not in existence. It held a crucifix and a mass-book and some rosaries, and Kate told me Miss Katharine's youngest and favorite brother had become a Roman Catholic while studying in Europe. It was a dreadful blow to the family; for in those sternly Protestant days there could have been few deeper disgraces to the Brandon family than to have one of its sons change his form of religion. Only Miss Katharine treated him with kindness, and after a time he disappeared without telling even her where he was going, and was only heard from indirectly once or twice afterward. It was a great grief to her. "And mamma knows," said Kate, "that she always had a lingering hope of his return or to hear that he was cloistered somewhere, for one of the last times she saw Aunt Katharine before she was ill, she spoke of soon going to be with all the rest, and said, 'Though your Uncle Henry, dear,' — and stopped and smiled sadly; 'you'll think me a very foolish old woman, but I never quite gave up thinking he might come home.'"

The Hall

Mrs. Kew did the honors of the lighthouse thoroughly on our first visit; but I think we rarely went to see her that we did not make some entertaining discovery. Mr. Kew's nephew, a smiling youth of forty, lived with them, and the two men were of a mechanical turn and had invented numerous aids to housekeeping, — appendages to the stove, and fixtures on the walls for everything that could be hung up; catches in the floor to hold the doors open, and ingenious apparatus to close them; but, above all, a system of barring and bolting for the wide "fore door," which would have disconcerted an energetic battering-ram. After all this work being expended, Mrs. Kew informed us that it was usually wide open all night in summer weather. On the back of this door I discovered one day a row of marks, and asked their significance. It seemed that Mrs. Kew had attempted one summer to keep count of the number of people who inquired about the depredations of the neighbors' chickens. Mrs. Kew's bedroom was partly devoted to the fine arts. There was a large collection of likenesses of her relatives and friends on the wall, which was interesting in the extreme. Mrs. Kew was always much pleased to tell their names, and her remarks about any feature not exactly perfect were very searching and critical. "That's my oldest brother's wife, Clorinthy Adams that was. She's well featured, if it were not for her nose, and that looks as if it had been thrown at her, and she was n't particular about having it on firm, in hopes of getting a better one. She sets by her looks, though."

There were often sailing-parties that came there from up and down the coast. One day Kate and I were spending the afternoon at the Light; we had been fishing, and were sitting in the doorway listening to a reminiscence of the winter Mrs. Kew kept school at the Four Corners; saw a boatful coming, and all lost our tempers. Mrs. Kew had a lame ankle, and Kate offered to go up with the visitors. There were some girls and young men who stood on the rocks awhile, and then asked us, with much better manners than the people who usually came, if they could see the lighthouse, and Kate led the way. She was dressed that day in a costume we both frequently wore, of gray skirts and blue sailor-jacket, and her boots were much the worse for wear. The celebrated Lancaster complexion was much darkened by the sun. Mrs. Kew expressed a wish to know what questions they would ask her, and I followed after a few minutes. They seemed to have finished asking about the lantern, and to have become personal.

"Don't you get tired staying here?"

"No, indeed!" said Kate.

"Is that your sister downstairs?"

"No, I have no sister."

"I should think you would wish she was. Are n't you ever lonesome?"

"Everybody is, sometimes," said Kate.

"But it's such a lonesome place!" said one of the girls. "I should think you would get work away. I live in Boston. Why, it's so awful quiet! nothing but the water, and the wind, when it blows; and I think either of them is worse than nothing. And only this little bit of a rocky place! I should want to go to walk."

I heard Kate pleasantly refuse the offer of pay for her services, and then they began to come down the steep stairs laughing and chattering with each other. Kate stayed behind to close the doors and leave everything all right, and the girl who had talked the most waited too, and when they were on the stairs just above me, and the others out of hearing, she said, "You're real good to show us the things. I guess you'll think I'm silly, but I do like you ever so much! I wish you would come to Boston. I 'm in a real nice store, — H——'s, on Winter Street ; and they 'll want new help in October. Perhaps you could be at my counter. I 'd teach you, and you could board with me. I 've got a real comfortable room, and I suppose I might have more things, for I get good pay ; but I like to send my money home to mother. I 'm at my aunt's now, but I am going back next Monday, and if you will tell me what your name is, I 'll find out for certain about the place, and write you. My name 's Mary Wendell."

I knew by Kate's voice that this had touched her. "You are very kind ; thank you ever so much," said she ; "but I cannot go and work with you. I should like to know you. I live in Boston too ; my friend and I are staying over in Deephaven for the summer only." She held out her hand to the girl, whose face had changed from its first expression of earnest good-humor to a very startled one ; and when she noticed Kate's hand, and a ring of hers, which had been turned round, she looked really frightened.

"Oh, will you please excuse me ?" said she, blushing. "I ought to have known better ; but you showed us round so willing, and I never thought of your not living here. I did n't mean to be rude."

"Of course you did not, and you were not. I am so glad you said it, and glad you like me," said Kate; and just then the party called the girl, and she hurried away, and I joined Kate. "Then you heard it all. That was worth having!" said she. "She was such a dear, honest little soul, and I mean to look for her when I get home."

Sometimes we used to go out to the Light early in the morning with the fishermen who went that way to the fishing-grounds, but we usually made the voyage early in the afternoon if it were not too hot, and we went fishing off the rocks or sat in the house with Mrs. Kew, who often related some of her Vermont experiences, or Mr. Kew would tell us surprising sea-stories and ghost-stories like a story-book sailor. Then we would have an unreasonably good supper, and afterward climb the ladder to the lantern to see the lamps lighted and sit there for a while watching the ships and the sunset. Almost all the coasters came in sight of Deephaven, and the sea outside the Light was their grand highway. Twice from the lighthouse we saw a yacht squadron like a flock of great white birds. As for the sunsets, it used to seem often as if we were near the heart of them, for the sea all around us caught the color of the clouds, and though the glory was wonderful, I remember best one still evening when there was a bank of heavy gray clouds in the west shutting down like a curtain, and the sea was silver-colored. You could look under and beyond the curtain of clouds into the palest, clearest yellow sky. There was a little black boat in the distance drifting slowly, climbing one white wave after another, as if it were bound out into that other world beyond. But presently the sun came from behind the clouds, and the dazzling golden light changed the look of everything, and it was the time then to say one thought it a beautiful sunset; while before one could only keep very still, and watch the boat, and wonder if heaven would not be somehow like that far, faint color, which was neither sea nor sky.

When we came down from the lighthouse and it grew late, we would beg for an hour or two longer on the water, and row away in the twilight far out from land, where, with our faces turned from the Light, it seemed as if we were alone, and the sea shoreless; and as the darkness closed round us softly, we watched the stars come out, and were always glad to see Kate's star and my star, which we had chosen when we were children. I used long ago to be sure of one thing, — that, however far away heaven might be, it could not be out of sight of the stars. Sometimes in the evening we waited out at sea for the moonrise, and then we would take the oars again and go slowly in, once in a while singing or talking, but oftenest silent.

My Lady Brandon and the Widow Jim

WHEN it was known that we had arrived in Deephaven, the people who had known Miss Brandon so well, and Mrs. Lancaster also, seemed to consider themselves Kate's friends by inheritance, and were most kind and friendly in either coming to see us or sending pleasant messages. Before the first week had ended we had no lack of society. They were not strangers to Kate to begin with, and as for me, I think it is easy for me to be contented, and to feel at home anywhere. I have the good fortune and the misfortune to belong to the navy,—

that is, my father does, — and my life has been consequently an unsettled one except during the years of my school life, when my friendship with Kate began.

I think I should be happy in any town if I were living there with Kate Lancaster. I will not praise my friend as I can praise her, or say half the things I might say honestly. She is so fresh and good and true, and enjoys life so heartily. She is so childlike, without being childish ; and I do not tell you that she is faultless, but when she makes mistakes she is sorrier and more ready to hopefully try again than any girl I know. Perhaps you would like to know something about us, but I am not writing Kate's biography and my own, only telling you of one summer which we spent together. Sometimes in Deephaven we were between six and seven years old, but at other times we have felt irreparably grown-up, and as if we carried a crushing weight of care and duty. In reality we are both twenty-four, and it is a pleasant age, though I think next year is sure to be pleasanter, for we do not mind growing older, since we have lost nothing that we mourn about, and are gaining so much. I shall be glad if you learn to know Kate a little in my stories. It is not that I am fond of her and endow her with imagined virtues and graces; no one can fail to see how unaffected she is, or not notice her thoughtfulness and generosity and her delightful fun, which never has a trace of coarseness or silliness. It was very pleasant having her for one's companion in such a place as Deephaven, for she has an unusual power of winning people's confidence, and of knowing with surest instinct how to meet them on their own ground. It is the girl's being so genuinely sympathetic and interested which makes every one ready to talk to her and be friends with her; just as the sunshine makes it easy for flowers to grow which the chilly winds hinder. She is not polite for the sake of seeming polite, but polite for the sake of being kind, and there is not a particle of what Hugh Miller justly calls the insolence of condescension about her; she is not brilliantly talented, yet she does everything in a charming fashion of her own; she is not profoundly learned, yet she knows much of which many wise people are ignorant, and while she is a patient scholar in both little things and great, she is no less a teacher to all her friends, — dear Kate Lancaster!

We found that we were considered Miss Brandon's representatives in Deephaven society, and this was no slight responsibility, as she had received much honor and respect. We heard again and again what a loss she had been to the town, and we tried that summer to do nothing to lessen the family reputation, and to give pleasure as well as take it, though we were singularly persistent in our pursuit of a good time. I grew much interested in what I heard of Miss Brandon, and it seems to me that it is a great privilege to have an elderly person in one's neighborhood, in town or country, who is proud, and conservative, and who lives in stately fashion; who is intolerant of sham and of useless novelties, and clings to the old ways of living and behaving as if they were part of her religion. There is something immensely respectable about such gentlewomen of the old school. They ignore all bustle and flashiness, and the conceit of the younger people, who act as if at last it had been time for them to appear and manage this world as it ought to have been managed before. Their position in modern society is much like that of the King's Chapel in its busy street in Boston; they stand for something assured and permanent. It perhaps might not have been easy to approach Miss Brandon, but it would have been impossible not to pay her great deference; it is a pleasure to think that she must have found this world a most polite world, and have had the highest opinion of its good manners. *Noblesse oblige:* that is true in more ways than one!

I cannot help wondering if those of us who will be left by and by to represent our own generation will seem to have such superior elegance of behavior; if we shall receive so much respect and be so much valued. It is hard to imagine it. We know that the world gains new refinements and a better culture; but to us there never will be such imposing ladies and gentlemen as those who belong to the old school.

The morning after we reached Deephaven we were busy upstairs, and there was a determined blow at the knocker of the front door. I went down to see who was there, and had the pleasure of receiving our first caller. She was a prim little old woman who looked pleased and expectant, who wore a neat cap and front, and whose eyes were as bright as black beads. She wore no bonnet, and had thrown a little three-cornered shawl, with palm-leaf figures, over her shoulders; and it was evident that she was a near neighbor. She was very short and straight and thin, and so quick that she darted like a pickerel when she moved about. It occurred to me at once that she was a very capable person, and had "faculty," and, dear me, how fast she talked! She hesitated a moment when she saw me, and dropped a fragment of a courtesy. "Miss Lanc'ster?" said she, doubtfully.

"No," said I, "I'm Miss Denis. Miss Lancaster is at home, though: come in, won't you?"

"O Mrs. Patton!" said Kate, who came down just then. "How very kind of you to come over so soon! I should have gone to see you to-day. I was asking Mrs. Kew last night if you were here."

"Land o' compassion!" said Mrs. Patton, as she shook Kate's hand delightedly. "Where'd ye s'pose I'd be, dear? I ain't like to move away from Deephaven now, after I've held by the place so long; I've got as many roots as the big ellum. Well, I should know you were a Brandon, no matter where I see you. You've got a real Brandon look; tall and straight, ain't you? It's four or five years since I saw you, except once at church, and once you went by, down to the shore, I s'pose. It was a windy day in the spring of the year."

"I remember it very well," said Kate.

"Those were both visits of only a day or two, and I was here at Aunt Katharine's funeral, and went away that same evening. Do you remember once I was here in the summer for a longer visit, five or six years ago, and I helped you pick currants in the garden? You had a very old mug."

"Now, who ever would ha' thought o' your rec'lecting that?" said Mrs. Patton. "Yes. I had that mug because it was handy to carry about among the bushes, and then I 'd empt' it into the basket as fast as I got it full. Your aunt always told me to pick all I wanted; she could n't use 'em, but they used to make sights o' currant wine in old times. I s'pose that mug would be considerable of a curiosity to anybody that was n't used to seeing it round. My grand'ther Joseph Toggerson — my mother was a Toggerson — picked it up on the long sands in a wad of sea-weed: strange it was n't broke, but it 's tough; I 've dropped it on the floor, many 's the time, and it ain't even chipped. There 's some Dutch reading on it, and it 's marked 1732. Now I should n't ha' thought you 'd remembered that old mug, I declare. Your aunt, she had a monstrous sight of chiny. She 's told me where 'most all of it come from, but I expect I 've forgot. My memory fails me a good deal by spells. If you had n't come down, I suppose your mother would have had the chiny packed up this spring, —

Mrs. Patton (The Widow Jim)

what she did n't take with her after your aunt died. S'pose she has n't made up her mind what to do with the house?"

"No," said Kate; "she wishes she could: it is a great puzzle to us."

"I hope you will find it in middling order," said Mrs. Patton, humbly. "Me and Mis' Dockum have done the best we knew,—opened the windows and let in the air, and tried to keep it from getting damp. I fixed all the woolens with fresh camphire and tobacco, the last o' the winter; you have to be dreadful careful in one o' these old houses, 'less everything gets creaking with moths in no time. Miss Katharine, how she did hate the sight of a moth-miller! There's something I'll speak about before I forget it: the mice have eat the backs of a pile o' old books that's stored away in the west chamber closet next to Miss Katharine's room, and I set a trap there, but it was older'n the ten commandments, that trap was, and the spring's rusty. I guess you'd better get some new ones and set round in different places, 'less the mice'll pester you. There ain't been no chance for 'em to get much of a living 'long through the winter, but they'll be sure to come back quick as they find there's likely to be good board. I see your aunt's cat setting out on the front steps. She never was no great of a mouser, but it went to my heart to see how pleased she looked! Come right back, did n't she? How they do hold to their old haunts!"

"Was that Miss Brandon's cat?" I asked, with great interest. "She has been up stairs with us, but I supposed she belonged to some neighbor, and had strayed in. She behaved as if she felt at home, poor old pussy!"

"We must keep her here," said Kate.

"Mis' Dockum took her after your mother went off, and Miss Katharine's maids," said Mrs. Patton; "but she told me that it was a long spell before she seemed to feel contented. She used to set on the steps and mew by the hour together, and try to get in, to first one door and then another. I used to think how bad Miss Katharine would feel; she set a great deal by a cat, and she took notice of this as long as she did of anything. Her mind failed her, you know. Great loss to Deephaven, she was. Proud woman, and some folks were scared of her; but I always got along with her, and I would n't ask for no kinder friend nor neighbor. I 've had my troubles, and I 've seen the day I was suffering poor, and I could n't have brought myself to ask town help nohow, but I wish ye 'd ha' heared her scold me when she found it out; and she come marching right into my kitchen door one morning, like a grenadier, and says she, 'Why did n't you send and tell me how sick and poor you are?' says she. And she said she 'd ha' been so glad to help me all along, but she thought I had means, — everybody did; and I see the tears in her eyes, but she was scolding me and speaking as if she was dreadful provoked. She made me comfortable herself, and she sent over one o' her maids to see to me, and got the doctor, and a load o' stuff come up from the store, so I did n't have to buy anything for a good many weeks. I got better and so 's to work, but she never 'd let me say nothing about it. I had a good deal o' trouble, and I thought I 'd lost my health, but I had n't, and that was thirty or forty years ago. There never was nothing going on at the great house that she did n't have me over, sewing or cleaning or company; and I got so that I knew how she liked to have things done. I felt as if it was my own sister, though I never had one, when I was going over to help lay her out. She used to talk as free to me as she would to Miss Lorimer or Miss Carew. I s'pose ye ain't seen nothing o' them yet? She was a good Christian woman, Miss Katharine was. 'The memory of the just is blessed;' that 's what Mr. Lorimer said in his sermon the Sunday after she died, and there was n't a blood-relation there to hear it. I declare it looked pitiful to see that pew empty that ought to ha' been the mourners' pew. Your mother, Mis' Lancaster, had to go home Saturday, your father was going away sudden to Washington, I 've understood, and she come back again the first of the week. There! it did n't make no sort o' difference, p'r'aps nobody thought of it but me. There had n't been anybody in the pew more than a couple o' times since she used to sit there herself, regular as Sunday come." And Mrs. Patton looked for a minute as if she were going to cry, but changed her mind upon second thought.

"Your mother gave me most of Miss Katharine's clothes; this cap belonged to her, that I 've got on now; it 's 'most wore out, but it does for mornings."

"Oh," said Kate, "I have two new ones for you in one of my trunks! Mamma meant to choose them herself, but she had not time, and so she told me, and I think I found the kind she thought you would like."

"Now I 'm sure!" said Mrs. Patton, "if that ain't kind; you don't tell me that Mis' Lancaster thought of me just as she was going off to sea? I shall set everything by them caps, and I 'm much obliged to you too, Miss

Kate. I was just going to speak of that time you were here and saw the mug; you trimmed a cap for Miss Katharine to give me, real Boston style. I guess that box of cap-fixings is up on the top shelf of Miss Katharine's closet now, to the left hand," said Mrs. Patton, with wistful certainty. "She used to make her every-day caps herself, and she had some beautiful materials laid away that she never used. Some folks has laughed at me for being so particular 'bout wearing caps except for best, but I don't know 's it 's presuming beyond my station, and somehow I feel more respect for myself when I have a good cap on. I can't get over your mother's rec'lecting about me; and she sent me a handsome present o' money this spring for looking after the house. I never should have asked for a cent; it 's a pleasure to me to keep an eye on it, out o' respect to your aunt. I was so pleased when I heard you were coming long o' your friend. I like to see the old place open; it was about as bad as having no meeting. I miss seeing the lights, and your aunt was a great hand for lighting up bright; the big hall lantern was lit every night, and she put it out when she went upstairs. She liked to go round same 's if it was day. You see I forget all the time she was sick, and go back to the days when she was well and about the house. When her mind was failing her, and she was upstairs in her room, her eyesight seemed to be lost part of the time, and sometimes she'd tell us to get the lamp and a couple o' candles in the middle o' the day, and then she'd be as satisfied! But she used to take a notion to set in the dark, some nights, and think, I s'pose. I should have forty fits, if I undertook it. That was a good while ago; and do you rec'lect how she used to play the piano? She used to be a great hand to play when she was young."

"Indeed, I remember it," said Kate, who told me afterward how her aunt used to sit at the piano in the twilight and play to herself. "She was formerly a skillful musician," said my friend, "though one would not have imagined she cared for music. When I was a child she used to play in company of an evening, and once when I was here one of her old friends asked for a tune, and she laughingly said that her day was over and her fingers were stiff; though I believe she might have played as well as ever then, if she had cared to try. But once in a while, when she had been quiet all day and rather sad,— I am ashamed that I used to think she was cross, — she would open the piano and sit there until late, while I used to be enchanted by her memories of dancing-tunes, and old psalms, and marches, and songs. There was one tune which I am sure had a history: there was a sweet, wild cadence in it, and she would come back to it again and again, always going through with it in the same measured way. I have remembered so many things about my aunt since I have been here," said Kate, "which I hardly noticed and did not understand when they happened. I was afraid of her when I was a little girl, but I think if I had grown up sooner, I should have enjoyed her heartily. It never used to occur to me that she had a spark of tenderness or of sentiment, until just before she was ill, but I have been growing more fond of her ever since. I might have given her a great deal more pleasure. It was not long after I was through school that she became so feeble, and of course she liked best having mamma come to see her; one of us had to be at home. I have thought lately how careful one ought to be, to be kind and thoughtful to one's old friends. It is so soon too late to be good to them, and then one is always so sorry."

I must tell you more of Mrs. Patton; of

Miss Brandon at her Piano

course, it was not long before we returned her visit, and we were much entertained; we always liked to see our friends in their own houses. Her house was a little way down the road, unpainted and gambrel-roofed, but so low that the old lilac-bushes which clustered round it were as tall as the eaves. The Widow Jim (as nearly every one called her in distinction to the Widow Jack Patton, who was a tailoress and lived at the other end of the town) was a very useful person. I suppose there must be her counterpart in all old New England villages. She sewed, and made elaborate rugs, and she had a decided talent for making carpets, — if there were one to be made, which must have happened seldom. But there were a great many to be turned and made over in Deephaven, and she went to the Carews' and Lorimers' at house-cleaning time or in seasons of great festivity. She had no equal in sickness, and knew how to brew every old-fashioned dose and to make every variety of herb-tea, and when her nursing was put to an end by her patient's death, she was commander-in-chief at the funeral, and stood near the doorway to direct the mourning friends to their seats; and I have no reason to doubt that she sometimes even had the immense responsibility of making out the order of the procession, since she had all genealogy and relationship at her tongue's end. It was an awful thing in Deephaven, we found, if the precedence was wrongly assigned, and once we chanced to hear some bitter remarks because the cousins of the departed wife had been placed after the husband's relatives, — "the blood-relations ridin' behind them that was only kin by marriage! I don't wonder they felt hurt!" said the person who spoke; a most unselfish and unassuming soul, ordinarily.

Mrs. Patton knew everybody's secrets, but she told them judiciously, if at all. She chattered all day to you, as a sparrow twitters, and you did not tire of her; and Kate and I were never more agreeably entertained than when she told us of old times and of Kate's ancestors and their contemporaries; for her memory was wonderful, and she had either seen everything that had happened in Deephaven for a long time, or had received the particulars from reliable witnesses. She had known much trouble; her husband had been but small satisfaction to her, and it was not to be wondered at if she looked upon all proposed marriages with compassion. She was always early at church, and she wore the same bonnet that she had worn when Kate was a child; it was such a well-preserved, proper, black straw bonnet, with discreet bows of ribbon, and a useful lace veil to protect it from the weather.

She showed us into the best room the first time we went to see her. It was the plainest little room, and very dull, and there was an exact sufficiency about its furnishings. Yet there was a certain dignity about it; it was unmistakably a best room, and not a place where one might make a litter or carry one's every-day work. You felt at once that somebody valued the prim old-fashioned chairs, and the two half-moon tables, and the thin carpet, which must have needed anxious stretching every spring to make it come to the edge of the floor. There were some mourning-pieces by way of decoration, inscribed with the names of Mrs. Patton's departed friends, — two worked in crewel to the memory of her father and mother, and two paper memorials, with the woman weeping under a willow at the side of a monument. They were all brown with age; and there was a sampler beside, worked by "Judith Beckett, aged ten," and all five were framed in slender black frames and hung very high on the walls. There was a rocking-chair which looked as if it felt too grand for use, and considered itself imposing. It tilted far back on its rockers, and was bent forward at the top to make one's head uncomfortable. It need not have troubled itself; nobody would ever wish to sit there. It was such a big rocking-chair, and Mrs. Patton was proud of it; always generously urging her guests to enjoy its comfort, which was imaginary with her, as she was so short that she could hardly have climbed into it without assistance, and then would have found herself off soundings, as the sailors say.

Mrs. Patton was a little ceremonious at first, but soon recovered herself and told us a great deal which we were glad to hear. I asked her once if she had not always lived at Deephaven. "Here and beyond East Parish," said she. "Mr. Patton, — that was my husband, — he owned a good farm there when I married him, but I come back here again after he died; place was all mortgaged; I never got a cent, and I was poorer than when I started. I worked harder 'n ever I did before or since to keep things together, but 't was n't any kind o' use. Your mother knows all about it, Miss Kate," — as if we might not be willing to believe it on her authority. "I come back here a widow and destitute, and I tell you the world looked fair to me when I left this house first to go over there. Don't you run no risks, you 're better off as you be, dears. But land sakes alive, 'he' did n't mean no hurt! and he set everything by me when he was himself. I don't make no scruples of speaking about it, everybody knows how it was, but I did go through with everything. I never knew what the day would bring forth," said the widow, as if this were the first time she had a chance to tell her sorrows to a sympathizing audience. She did not seem to mind talking about the troubles of her married life any more than a soldier minds telling the story of his campaigns, and dwells with pride on the worst battle of all.

Her favorite subject always was Miss Brandon, and after a pause she said that she hoped we were finding everything right in the house; she had meant to take up the carpet in the best spare room, but it did n't seem to need it; it was taken up the year before, and the room had not been used since; there was not a mite of dust under it last time. And Kate assured her, with an appearance of great wisdom, that she did not think it could be necessary at all.

"I come home and had a good cry yesterday after I was over to see you," said Mrs.

Patton, and I could not help wondering if she really could cry, for she looked so perfectly dried up, so dry that she might rustle in the wind. "Your aunt had been failin' so long that just after she died it was a relief, but I 've got so 's to forget all about that, and I miss her as she used to be; it seemed as if you had stepped into her place, and you look some as she used to when she was young."

"You must miss her," said Kate, "and I know how much she used to depend upon you. You were very kind to her."

"I watched with her the night she died," said the widow, with mournful satisfaction. "I have lived neighbor to her all my life except the thirteen years I was married, and there was n't a week I was n't over to the great house except I was off to a distance taking care of the sick. When she got to be feeble she always wanted me to 'tend to the cleaning and to see to putting the canopies and curtains on the bedsteads, and she would n't trust nobody but me to handle some of the best china. I used to say, 'Miss Katharine, why don't you have some young folks come and stop with you? There's Mis' Lancaster's daughter a growing up'; but she did n't seem to care for nobody but your mother. You would n't believe what a hand she used

The Graveyard

to be for company in her younger days. Surprisin' how folks alters! When I first rec'lect her much she was as straight as an arrow, and she used to go to Boston visiting and come home with the top of the fashion. She always did dress elegant. It used to be gay here, and she was always going down to the Lorimers' or the Carews' to tea, and they coming here. Her sister was married; she was a good deal older; but some of her brothers were at home. There was your grandfather and Mr. Henry. I don't think she ever got it over, — his disappearing so. There were lots of folks then that's dead and gone, and they used to have their card-parties, and old Cap'n Manning — he's dead and gone — used to have 'em all to play whist every fortnight, sometimes three or four tables, and they always had cake and wine handed round, or the cap'n made some punch, like's not, with oranges in it, and lemons; *he* knew how! He was a bachelor to the end of his days, the old cap'n was, but he used to entertain real handsome. I rec'lect one night they was a playin' after the wine was brought in, and he upset his glass all over Miss Martha Lorimer's invisible-green watered silk, and spoilt the better part of two breadths. She sent right over for me early the next morning to see if I knew of anything to take out the spots, but I did n't, though I can take grease out o' most any material. We tried clear alcohol, and saleratus-water, and hartshorn, and pouring water through, and heating of it, and when we got through it was worse than when we started. She felt dreadful bad about it, and at last she says, 'Judith, we won't work over it any more, but if you 'll give me a day some time or 'nother, we 'll rip it up and make a quilt of it.' I see that quilt last time I was in Miss Rebecca's north chamber. Miss Martha was her aunt; you never saw her; she was dead and gone before your day. It was a silk old Cap'n Peter Lorimer, her brother, who left 'em his money, brought home from sea, and she had worn it for best and second best eleven year. It looked as good as new, and she never would have ripped it up if she could have matched it. I said it seemed to be a shame, but it was a curi's figure. Cap'n Manning fetched her one to pay for it the next time he went to Boston. She did n't want to take it, but he would n't take no for an answer; he was freehanded, the cap'n was. I helped 'em make it 'long of Mary Ann Simms the dress-maker, — she 's dead and gone too, — the time it was made. It was brown, and a beautiful-looking piece, but it wore shiny, and she made a double-gown of it before she died."

Mrs. Patton brought Kate and me some delicious old-fashioned cake with much spice in it, and told us it was made by old Mrs. Chantrey Brandon's receipt which came from England, that it would keep a year, and she always kept a loaf by her, now that she could afford it; she supposed we knew Miss Katharine had named her in her will long before she was sick. "It has put me beyond fear of want," said Mrs. Patton. "I won't deny that I used to think it would go hard with me when I got so old I could n't earn my living. You see I never laid up but a little, and it 's hard for a woman who comes of respectable folks to be dependent in her last days; but your aunt, Miss Kate, she thought of it too, and I 'm sure I 'm thankful to be so comfortable, and to stay in my house, which I could n't have done, like 's not. Miss Rebecca Lorimer said to me after I got news of the will, 'Why, Mis' Patton, you don't suppose your friends would ever have let you want!' And I says, 'My friends are kind, — the Lord bless 'em! — but I feel better to be able to do for myself than to be beholden.' "

After this long call we went down to the

post-office, and coming home stopped for a while in the old burying-ground, which we had noticed the day before; and we sat for the first time on the great stone in the wall, in the shade of a maple-tree, where we so often waited afterward for the stage to come with the mail, or rested on our way home from a walk. It was a comfortable perch; we used sometimes to read our letters there, I remember.

I must tell you a little about the Deephaven burying-ground, for its interest was inexhaustible, and I do not know how much time we may have spent in reading the long epitaphs on the gravestones and trying to puzzle out the inscriptions, which were often so old and worn that we could only trace a letter here and there. It was a neglected corner of the world, and there were straggling sumachs and acacias scattered about the inclosure, while a row of fine old elms marked the boundary of two sides. The grass was long and tangled, and most of the stones leaned one way or the other, and some had fallen flat. There were a few handsome old family monuments clustered in one corner, among which the one that marked Miss Brandon's grave looked so new and fresh that it seemed inappropriate. "It should have been dingy to begin with, like the rest," said Kate one day; "but I think it will make itself look like its neighbors as soon as possible."

There were many stones which were sacred to the memory of men who had been lost at sea, almost always giving the name of the departed ship, which was so kept in remembrance; and one felt as much interest in the ship Starlight, supposed to have foundered off the Cape of Good Hope, as in the poor fellow who had the ill luck to be one of her crew. There were dozens of such inscriptions; and there were other stones perpetuating the fame of Honourable gentlemen who had been members of His Majesty's Council, or surveyors of His Majesty's Woods, or King's Officers of Customs for the town of Deephaven. Some of the epitaphs were beautiful, showing that tenderness for the friends who had died, that longing to do them justice, to fully acknowledge their virtues and dearness, which is so touching, and so unmistakable even under the stiff, quaint expressions and formal words. We often used to notice names, and learn their history from the old people whom we knew, and in this way we heard many stories which we never shall forget. It is wonderful, the romance and tragedy and adventure which one may find in a quiet old-fashioned country town; though to heartily enjoy the every-day life one must care to study life and character, and must find pleasure in thought and observation of simple things, and have an instinctive, delicious interest in what to other eyes is unflavored dullness.

To go back to Mrs. Patton; on our way home, after our first call upon her, we stopped to speak to Mrs. Dockum, who mentioned that she had seen us going in to the "Widow Jim's."

"Willin' woman," said Mrs. Dockum, "always been respected; got an uncommon facility o' speech. I never saw such a hand to talk, but then she has something to say, which ain't the case with everybody. Good neighbor, does according to her means always. Dreadful tough time of it with her husband, shif'less and drunk all his time. Noticed that dent in the side of her forehead, I s'pose? That 's where he liked to have killed her; slung a stone bottle at her."

"*What!*" said Kate and I, very much shocked.

"She don't like to have it inquired about; but she and I were sitting up with 'Manda Damer one night, and she gave me the particulars. I knew he did it, for she had a fit

Mrs. Dockum

o' sickness afterward. Had sliced cucumbers for breakfast that morning; he was very partial to them, and he wanted some vinegar. Happened to be two bottles in the cellar-way just alike, and one of 'em was vinegar and the other had sperrit in it at haying-time. He takes up the wrong one and pours on quick, and out come the hayseed and flies, and he give the bottle a sling, and it hit her there where you see the scar; might put the end of your finger into the dent. He said he meant to break the bottle ag'in the door, but it went slantwise, sort of. I don' know, I 'm sure" (meditatively). "She said he was good-natured; it was early in the mornin', and he had n't had time to get upset; but he had a high temper naturally, and so much drink had n't made it much better. She had good prospects when she married him. Six-foot-two and red cheeks and straight as a Noroway pine; had a good property from his father, and his mother come of a good family, but he died in debt; drank like a fish. Yes, 't was a shame, nice woman; good consistent church-member; always been respected; useful among the sick."

Deephaven Society

IT was curious to notice, in this quaint little fishing-village by the sea, how clearly the gradations of society were defined. The place prided itself most upon having been long ago the residence of one Governor Chantrey, who was a rich ship-owner and East India merchant, and whose fame and magnificence were almost fabulous. It was a never-ceasing regret that his house should have burned down after he died, and there is no doubt that if it were still standing it would rival any ruin of the Old World.

The elderly people, though laying claim to no slight degree of present consequence, modestly ignored it, and spoke with pride of the grand way in which life was carried on by their ancestors, the Deephaven families of old times. I think Kate and I were assured at least a hundred times that Governor Chantrey kept a valet, and his wife, Lady Chantrey, kept a lady's maid and a housekeeper, and that the governor had an uncle in England who was a lord; and I believe this must have been why our friends felt so deep an interest in the affairs of the English nobility; they no doubt felt themselves entitled to seats near the throne itself. There were formerly five families who kept their coaches in Deephaven; there were balls at the governor's, and regal entertainments at other of the grand mansions; there were twenty college men, young and old, in the Sunday congregation; there is not a really distinguished person in the country who will not prove to have been directly or indirectly connected with Deephaven. We were shown the cellar of the Chantrey house, and the terraces, and a few clumps of lilacs, and the grand rows of elms. There are still two of the governor's warehouses left, but his ruined wharves are fast disappearing, and are almost deserted, except by small barefooted boys who sit on their edges to fish for sea-perch when the tide comes in. There is an imposing monument in the burying-ground to the great man and his amiable consort. I am sure that if there were any surviving relatives of the governor, they would receive in Deephaven far more deference than is consistent with the principles of a republican government; but the family became extinct long since, and I have heard, though it is not a subject that one may speak of lightly, that the sons were unworthy their noble descent and came to inglorious ends.

There were still remaining a few representatives of the old families, who were treated with much reverence by the rest of the townspeople, although they were, like the conies of Scripture, a feeble folk.

Deephaven is utterly out of fashion. It never recovered from the effects of the embargo of 1807, and a sand-bar has been steadily filling in the mouth of the harbor. Though the fishing gives what occupation there is for the inhabitants of the place, it is by no means sufficient to draw recruits from abroad. But nobody in Deephaven cares for excitement; and if some one once in a while has the low taste to prefer a more active life, he is obliged to go elsewhere in search of it, and is spoken of afterward with kind pity. I well remember the Widow Moses said to me, in speaking of a certain misguided nephew of hers, "I never could see what could 'a' sot him out to leave so many privileges and go way off to Lynn, with all them children, too. Why, they lived here no more than a cable's length from the meetin'-house!"

There were two schooners owned in town, and 'Bijah Mauley and Jo Sands each owned a trawl. There were some schooners and a small brig slowly going to pieces by the wharves, and indeed Deephaven looked more or less out of repair. All along shore one might see dories and wherries and whale-boats, which had been left to die a lingering death. There is something piteous to me in the sight of an old boat. If one I had used much and cared for were past its usefulness, I should say good-by to it, and have it towed out to sea and sunk; it never should be left to fall to pieces above high-water mark.

Even the fishermen felt a satisfaction, and seemed to realize their privilege, in being residents of Deephaven; but among the nobility and gentry there lingered a fierce pride in their family and town records, and a hardly concealed contempt and pity for people who were obliged to live in other parts of the world. There were acknowledged to be a few disadvantages, such as living nearly a dozen miles from the railway; but, as Miss Honora Carew said, the tone of Deephaven society had always been very high, and it was very nice that there had never been any manufacturing element introduced. She could not feel too grateful, herself, that there was no disagreeable foreign population.

"But," said Kate one day, "would n't you like to have some pleasant new people brought into town?"

"Certainly, my dear," said Miss Honora, rather doubtfully; "I have always been public-spirited; but then, we always have guests in summer, and I am growing old. I should not care to enlarge my acquaintance to any great extent." Miss Honora and Mrs. Dent had lived gay lives in their younger days, and were interested and connected with the outside world more than any of our Deephaven friends; but they were quite contented to stay in their own house, with their books and letters and knitting, and they carefully read Littell, the Spectator, and "the new magazine," as they called the Atlantic.

The Carews were very intimate with the minister and his sister, and there were one or two others who belonged to this set.

There was Mr. Joshua Dorsey, who wore his hair in a queue, was very deaf, and carried a ponderous cane which had belonged to his venerated father, — a much taller man than he. He was polite to Kate and me, but we never knew him much. He went to play whist with the Carews every Monday evening, and commonly went out fishing once a week. He had begun the practice of law, but he had lost his hearing, and at the same time his lady-love had inconsiderately fallen in love with somebody else; after which he retired from active business life. He had a fine library, which he invited us once to examine. He had many new books, but they looked shockingly overdressed, in their fresher bindings, beside the old brown volumes of essays and sermons, and lighter works in many-volume editions.

A prominent link in society was Widow Tully, who had been the much-respected housekeeper of old Captain Manning for forty years. When he died he left her the use of his house and family pew, besides an annuity. The existence of Mr. Tully seemed to be a myth. During the first of his widow's residence in town she had been much affected when obliged to speak of him, and always represented herself as having seen better days and as being highly connected. But she was apt to be ungrammatical when excited, and there was a whispered tradition that she used to keep a toll-bridge in a town in Connecticut ; though the mystery of her previous state of existence will probably never be solved. She wore mourning for the captain which would have befitted his widow, and patronized the townspeople conspicuously, while she herself was treated with much condescension by the Carews and Lorimers. She occupied, on the whole, much the same position that Mrs. Betty Barker did in Cranford. And, indeed, Kate and I were often reminded of that estimable town. We heard that Kate's aunt, Miss Brandon, had never been appreciative of Mrs. Tully's merits, and that since her death the others had received Mrs. Tully into their society rather more.

Widow Tully

It seemed as if all the clocks in Deephaven, and all the people with them, had stopped years ago, and the people had been doing over and over what they had been busy about during the last week of their unambitious progress. Their clothes had lasted wonderfully well, and they had no need to earn money when there was so little chance to spend it; indeed, there were several families who seemed to have no more visible means of support than a balloon. There were no young people whom we knew, though a number used to come to church on Sunday from the inland farms, or "the country," as we learned to say. There were children among the fishermen's families at the shore, but a few years will see Deephaven possessed by two classes instead of the time-honored three.

As for our first Sunday at church, it must be in vain to ask you to imagine our delight when we heard the tuning of a bass-viol in the gallery just before service. We pressed each other's hands most tenderly, looked up at the singers' seats, and then trusted ourselves to look at each other. It was more than we had hoped for. There was also a violin and sometimes a flute, and a choir of men and women singers, though the congregation were expected to join in the psalm-singing. The first hymn was

> "The Lord our God is full of might,
> The winds obey his will,"

to the tune of St. Ann's. It was all so delightfully old-fashioned; our pew was a square pew, and was by an open window looking seaward. We also had a view of the entire congregation; and as we were somewhat early, we watched the people come in, with great interest. The Deephaven aristocracy came with stately step up the aisle; this was all the chance there was for displaying their unquestioned dignity in public.

Many of the people drove to church in wagons that were low and old and creaky, with worn buffalo-robes over the seat, and some hay tucked underneath for the sleepy, undecided old horse. Some of the younger farmers and their wives had high, shiny wagons, with tall horsewhips, — which they sometimes brought into church, — and they drove up to the steps with a consciousness of being conspicuous and enviable. They had a bashful look when they came in, and for a few minutes after they took their seats they evidently felt that all eyes were fixed upon them; but after a little while they were quite at their ease, and looked critically at the new arrivals.

The old folks interested us most. "Do you notice how many more old women there are than old men?" whispered Kate to me. And we wondered if the husbands and brothers had been drowned, and if it must not be sad to look at the blue, sunshiny sea beyond the marshes, if the far-away white sails reminded them of some ships that had never sailed home into Deephaven harbor, or of fishing-boats that had never come back to land.

The girls and young men adorned themselves in what they believed to be the latest fashion, but the elderly women were usually relics of old times in manner and dress. They wore to church thin, soft silk gowns that must have been brought from over the seas years upon years before, and wide collars fastened with mourning-pins holding a lock of hair. They had big black bonnets, some of them with stiff capes, such as Kate and I had not seen before since our childhood. They treasured large rusty lace veils of scraggly pattern, and wore sometimes, on pleasant Sundays, white China crape shawls with attenuated fringes; and there were two or three of these shawls in the congregation which had been dyed black, and gave an aspect of meekness and general unworthiness to the aged wearer, they clung and drooped about the figure in such a hopeless way. We used to notice often the most interesting scarfs, without which no Deephaven woman considered herself in full dress. Sometimes there were red India scarfs in spite of its being hot weather; but our favorite ones were long strips of silk, embroidered along the edges and at the ends with dismal-colored floss in odd patterns. I think there must have been a fashion once, in Deephaven, of working these scarfs, and I should not be surprised to find that it was many years before the fashion of working samplers came about. Our friends always wore black mitts on warm Sundays, and many of them carried neat little bags of various designs on their arms, containing a precisely folded pocket-handkerchief, and a frugal lunch of caraway seeds or red and white peppermints. I should like you to see, with your own eyes, Widow Ware and Miss Exper'ence Hull, two old sisters whose personal appearance we delighted in, and whom we saw feebly approaching down the street this first Sunday morning under the shadow of the two last members of an otherwise extinct race of parasols.

There were two or three old men who sat near us. They were sailors, — there is some-

The Sunday Dinner

thing unmistakable about a sailor, — and they had a curiously ancient, uncanny look, as if they might have belonged to the crew of the Mayflower, or even have cruised about with the Northmen in the times of Harald Harfaager and his comrades. They had been blown about by so many winter winds, so browned by summer suns, and wet by salt spray, that their hands and faces looked like leather, with a few deep folds instead of wrinkles. They had pale blue eyes, very keen and quick; their hair looked like the fine seaweed which clings to the kelp-roots and mussel-shells in little locks. These friends of ours sat solemnly at the heads of their pews and looked unflinchingly at the minister, when they were not dozing, and they sang with voices like the howl of the wind, with an occasional deep note or two.

Have you never seen faces that seemed old-fashioned? Many of the people in Deephaven church looked as if they must be — if not supernaturally old — exact copies of their remote ancestors. I wonder if it is not possible that the features and expression may be almost perfectly reproduced. These faces were not modern American faces, but belonged rather to the days of the early settlement of the country, the old colonial times.

We often heard quaint words and expressions which we never had known anywhere else but in old books. There was a great deal of sea-lingo in use; indeed, we learned a great deal ourselves, unconsciously, and used it afterwards to the great amusement of our friends; but there were also many peculiar provincialisms, and among the people who lived on the lonely farms inland we often noticed words we had seen in Chaucer, and studied out at school in our English literature class. Everything in Deephaven was more or less influenced by the sea; the minister spoke oftenest of Peter and his fishermen companions, and prayed most earnestly every Sunday morning for those who go down to the sea in ships. He made frequent allusions and drew numberless illustrations of a similar kind for his sermons, and indeed I am in doubt whether, if the Bible had been written wholly in inland countries, it would have been much valued in Deephaven.

The singing was very droll, for there was a majority of old voices, which had seen their best days long before, and the bass-viol was excessively noticeable, and apt to be a little ahead of the time the singers kept, while the violin lingered after. Somewhere on the other side of the church we heard an acute voice which rose high above all the rest of the congregation, sharp as a needle, and slightly cracked, with a limitless supply of breath. It rose and fell gallantly, and clung long to the high notes of Dundee. It was like the wail of the banshee, which sounds clear to the fated hearer above all other noises. We afterward became acquainted with the owner of this voice, and were surprised to find her a meek widow, who was like a thin black beetle in her pathetic cypress veil and big black bonnet. She looked as if she had forgotten who she was, and spoke with an apologetic whine; but we heard she had a temper as high as her voice, and as much to be dreaded as the equinoctial gale.

Near the church was the parsonage, where Mr. Lorimer lived, and the old Lorimer house not far beyond was occupied by Miss Rebecca Lorimer. Some stranger might ask the question why the minister and his sister did not live together, but you would have understood it at once after you had lived for a while in town. They were very fond of each other, and the minister dined with Miss Rebecca on Sundays, and she passed the day with him on Wednesdays, and they ruled their separate households with decision and dignity. I think Mr. Lorimer's house showed no signs of being without a mistress, any more than his sister's betrayed the want of a master's care and authority.

The Carews were very kind friends of ours, and had been Miss Brandon's best friends. We heard that there had always been a coolness between Miss Brandon and Miss Lorimer, and, that, though they exchanged visits and were always polite, there was a chill in the politeness, and one would never have suspected them of admiring each other at all. We had the whole history of the trouble, which dated back scores of years, from Miss Honora Carew; but we always took pains to appear ignorant of the feud, and I think Miss Lorimer was satisfied that it was best not to refer to it, and to let bygones be bygones. It would not have been true Deephaven courtesy to prejudice Kate against her grand-aunt, and Miss Rebecca cherished her dislike in silence, which gave us a most grand respect for her, since we knew she thought herself in the right; though I think it never had come to an open quarrel between these majestic ladies.

Miss Honora Carew and Mr. Dick Carew and their elder sister, Mrs. Dent, had a charmingly sedate and quiet home in the old Carew house. Mrs. Dent was ill a great deal while we were there, but she must have been a very brilliant woman, and was not at all dull when we knew her. She had outlived her husband and her children, and she had, several years before our summer there, given up her own home, which was in the city, and had come back to Deephaven. Miss Honora — dear Miss Honora! — had been one of the brightest, happiest girls, and had lost none of her brightness and happiness by growing old. She had lost none of her fondness for society, though she was so contented in quiet Deephaven, and I think she enjoyed Kate's and my stories of our pleasures as much as we did hers of old times. We used to go to see her almost every day. "Mr. Dick," as they called their brother, had once been a merchant in the East Indies, and there were quantities of curiosities and most beautiful china which he had brought and sent home, which gave the house a character of its own. He had been very rich, and had lost some of his money, and afterward came home, and was still considered to possess princely wealth by his neighbors. He had a great fondness for reading and study, which had not been lost sight of during his business life, and he spent most of his time in his library. He and Mr. Lorimer had their differences of opinion about certain points of theology, and this made them much fonder of each other's society, and gave them a great deal of pleasure; for after every series of arguments, each was sure that he had vanquished the other, or there were alternate victories and defeats which made life vastly interesting and important.

Miss Carew and Mrs. Dent had a great treasury of old brocades and laces and ornaments, which they showed us one day, and told us stories of the wearers; or if they were their own, there were always some reminiscences which they liked to talk over with each other and with us. I never shall forget the first evening we took tea with them; it impressed us very much, and yet nothing wonderful happened. Tea was handed round by an old-fashioned maid, and afterward we sat talking in the twilight, looking out at the garden. It was such a delight to have tea served in this way. I wonder that the fashion has been almost forgotten. Kate and I took much pleasure in choosing our tea-poys; hers had a mandarin parading on the top, and mine a flight of birds and a pagoda; and we often used them afterward,

Mr. Dick and Mr. Lorimer

for Miss Honora asked us to come to tea whenever we liked. "A stupid, common country town," some one dared to call Deephaven in a letter once, and how bitterly we resented it! That was a house where one might always find the best society and the most charming manners and good-breeding; and if I were asked to tell you what I mean by the word "lady," I should ask you to go, if it were possible, to call upon Miss Honora Carew.

After a while the elder sister said, "My dears, we always have prayers at nine, for I have to go up stairs early nowadays." And then the servants came in, and she read solemnly the King of glory psalm, which I have always liked best; and then Mr. Dick read the church prayers, the form of prayer to be used in families. We stayed later to talk with Miss Honora after we had said good night to Mrs. Dent. And we told each other, as we went home in the moonlight down the quiet street, how much we had enjoyed the evening; for somehow the house and the people had nothing to do with the present, or the hurry of modern life. I have never heard that psalm since without its bringing back that summer night in Deephaven, the beautiful quaint old room,—and Kate and I feeling so young and worldly by contrast,—the flickering, shaded light of the candles, the old book, and the voices that said Amen.

There were several other fine old houses in Deephaven beside this and the Brandon house, though that was rather the most imposing. There were two or three which had not been kept in repair, and were deserted, and of course they were said to be haunted, and we were told of their ghosts, and why they walked, and when. From some of the local superstitions Kate and I have vainly endeavored ever since to shake ourselves free. There was a most heathenish fear of doing certain things on Friday, and there were countless signs in which we still have confidence. When the moon is very bright and other people grow sentimental, we only remember that it is a fine night to catch hake.

The Captains

I SHOULD consider my account of Deephaven society incomplete if I did not tell you something of the ancient mariners, who may be found every pleasant morning sunning themselves like turtles on one of the wharves. Sometimes there was a considerable group of them; but the less constant members of the club were older than the rest, and the epidemics of rheumatism in town were sadly frequent. We found that it was etiquette to call them each captain, but I think some of the Deephaven men took the title by brevet upon arriving at a proper age.

They sat close together because so many

of them were deaf; and when we were lucky enough to overhear the conversation, it seemed to concern their adventures at sea, or the freight carried out by the Sea Duck, the Ocean Rover, or some other Deephaven ship, — the particulars of the voyage and its disasters and successes being as familiar as the wanderings of the children of Israel to an old parson. There were sometimes violent altercations when the captains differed as to the tonnage of some craft that had been a prey to the winds and waves, dry-rot, or barnacles fifty years before. The old fellows puffed away at little black pipes with short stems, and otherwise consumed tobacco in fabulous quantities. It is needless to say that they gave an immense deal of attention to the weather. We used to wish we could join this agreeable company; but we found that the appearance of an outsider caused a disapproving silence, and that the meeting was evidently not to be interfered with. Once we were impertinent enough to hide ourselves for a while just round the corner of the warehouse; but we were afraid or ashamed to try it again, though the conversation was inconceivably edifying. Captain Isaac Horn, the eldest and wisest of all, was discoursing upon some cloth he had purchased once in

Bristol, which the shopkeeper delayed sending until just as they were ready to weigh anchor.

"I happened to take a look at that cloth," said the captain, in a loud droning voice, "and as quick as I got sight of it, I spoke onpleasant of that swindling English fellow, and the crew, they stood back. I was dreadful high-tempered in them days, mind ye, and I had the gig manned. We was out in the stream, just ready to sail. 'T was no use waiting any longer for the wind to change, and we was going north-about. I went ashore, and when I walks into his shop ye never see a creatur' so wilted. Ye see the miser'ble sculpin thought I 'd never stop to open the goods, an' it was a chance I did, mind ye! 'Lor,' says he, grinning and turning the color of a biled lobster, 'I s'posed ye were a-standing out to sea by this time.' 'No,' says I, 'and I 've got my men out here on the quay a-landing that cloth o' yourn; and if you don't send just what I bought and paid for down there to go back in the gig within fifteen minutes, I 'll take ye by the collar and drop ye into the dock.' I was twice the size of him, mind ye, and master strong. 'Don't ye like it?' says he, edging round; 'I'll change it for ye, then.' Ter'ble perlite he was. 'Like it?' says I, 'it looks as if it were built of dog's hair and divil's wool, kicked together by spiders; and it's coarser than Irish frieze; three threads to an *armful*,' says I."

This was evidently one of the captain's favorite stories, for we heard an approving grumble from the audience.

In the course of a walk inland we made a new acquaintance, Captain Lant, whom we had noticed at church, and who sometimes joined the company on the wharf. We had been walking through the woods, and coming out to his fields we went on to the house for some water. There was no one at home but the captain, who told us cheerfully that he should be pleased to serve us, though his women-folks had gone off to a funeral, the other side of the P'int. He brought out a pitcherful of milk; and after we had drunk some, we all sat down together in the shade. The captain brought an old flag-bottomed chair from the woodhouse, and sat down facing Kate and me, with an air of certainty that he was going to hear something new and make some desirable new acquaintances, and also that he could tell something it would be worth our while to hear. He looked more and more like a well-to-do old English sparrow, and chippered faster and faster.

"Queer ye should know I'm a sailor so quick; why, I've been a-farming it this twenty years; have to go down to the shore and take a day's fishing every hand's turn, though, to keep the old hulk clear of barnacles. There! I do wish I lived nigher the shore, where I could see the folks I know, and talk about what's been a-goin' on. You don't know anything about it, you don't; but it's tryin' to a man to be called 'old Cap'n Lant,' and, so to speak, be forgot when there's anything stirring, and be called gran'ther by clumsy creatur's goin' on fifty and sixty, who can't do no more work to-day than I can; an' then the women-folks keeps a-tellin' me to be keerful and not fall, and as how I'm too old to go out fishing; and when they want to be soft-spoken, they say as how they don't see as I fail, and how wonderful I keep my hearin'. I never did want to farm it, but 'she' always took it to heart when I was off on a v'y'ge, and this farm and some consider'ble means beside come to her from her brother, and they all sot to and give me no peace of mind till I sold out my share of the Ann Eliza and come ashore for good. I did keep an eighth of the Pactolus, and I was ship's husband for a long spell, but she never was heard from on her last voyage to Singapore. I was the lonesomest man, when I first come ashore, that ever you see. Well, you are master hands to walk, if you come way up from the Brandon house. I wish the women was at home. Know Miss Brandon? Why, yes; and I remember all her brothers and sisters, and her father and mother. I can see 'em now coming into meeting, proud as Lucifer and straight as a mast, every one of 'em. Miss Katharine, she always had her butter from this very farm. Some of the folks used to go down every Saturday; and my wife, she 's been in the house a hundred times, I s'pose. So you are Hathaway Brandon's grand-daughter?" (to Kate); "why, him and me have been out fishing together many 's the time, — he and Chantrey, his next younger brother. Henry, he was a disapp'intment; he went to furrin parts and never come back again, I s'pose you 've heard? I never was so set ag'in Mr. Henry as some folks was. He was the pleasantest spoken of the whole on 'em. You do look like the Brandons; you really favor 'em consider'ble. Well, I 'm pleased to see ye, I 'm sure."

We asked him many questions about the old people, and found he knew all the family histories and told them with great satisfac-

The Old Captains

tion. We found he had his pet stories, and it must have been gratifying to have an entirely new and fresh audience. He was adroit in leading the conversation around to a point where the stories would come in appropriately, and we helped him as much as possible. In a small neighborhood, all the people know each other's stories and experiences by heart, and I have no doubt the old captain had been disregarded many times on the occasion of beginning a favorite anecdote. There was a story which he told us that first day, which he assured us was strictly true, and it is certainly a remarkable instance of the influence of one mind upon another at a distance. It seems to me worth preserving, at any rate; and as we heard it from the old man, with his solemn voice and serious expression and quaint gestures, it was singularly impressive.

"When I was a youngster," said Captain Lant, "I was an orphan, and I was bound out to old Mr. Peletiah Daw's folks, over on the Ridge Road. It was in the time of the last war, and he had a nephew, Ben Dighton, a dreadful high-strung, wild fellow, who had gone off on a privateer. The old man, he set everything by Ben; he would disoblige his own boys any day to please him. This was in his latter days, and he used to have spells of wandering and being out of his head; and he used to call for Ben and talk sort of foolish about him, till they would tell him to stop. Ben never did a stroke of work for him, either; but he was a handsome fellow, and had a way with him when he was good-natured. One night old Peletiah had been very bad all day, and was getting quieted down, and it was after supper; we sat round in the kitchen, and he lay in the bedroom opening out. There were some pitch-knots blazing, and the light shone in on the bed, and all of a sudden something made me look up and look in; and there was the old man setting up straight, with his eyes shining at me like a cat's. 'Stop 'em!' says he; '*stop 'em!*' and his two sons run in then to catch hold of him, for they thought he was beginning with one of his wild spells; but he fell back on the bed and began to cry like a baby. 'Oh, dear me,' says he, 'they 've hung him, — hung him right up to the yard-arm! Oh, they ought n't to have done it; cut him down quick! he did n't think; he means well, Ben does; he was only hasty. O my God, I can't bear to see him swing round by the neck! There 's poor Ben hung up to the yard-arm. Let me alone, I say!' Andrew and Moses, they were holding him with all their might, and they were both hearty men; but he 'most got away from them once or twice, and he screeched and howled like a mad creatur', and then he would cry again like a child. He was worn out after a while and lay back quiet, and said over and over, 'Poor Ben!' and 'hung at the yard-arm;' and he told the neighbors next day, but nobody noticed him much, and he seemed to forget it as his mind come back. All that summer he was miser'ble, and towards cold weather he failed right along, though he had been a master strong man in his day, and his timbers held together well. Along late in the fall he had taken to his bed, and one day there came to the house a fellow named Sim Decker, a reckless fellow he was, too, who had gone out in the same ship with Ben. He pulled a long face when he came in, and said he had brought bad news. They had been taken prisoner and carried into port and put in jail, and Ben Dighton had got a fever there and died.

"'You lie!' says the old man from the bedroom, speaking as loud and f'erce as ever you heard. 'They hung him to the yard-arm!'

"'Don't mind him,' says Andrew; 'he's

wandering-like, and he had a bad dream along back in the spring; I s'posed he'd forgotten it.' But the Decker fellow, he turned pale, and kept talking crooked while he listened to old Peletiah a-scolding to himself. He answered the questions the women-folks asked him, — they took on a good deal, — but pretty soon he got up and winked to me and Andrew, and we went out in the yard. He begun to swear, and then says he, 'When did the old man have his dream?' Andrew could n't remember, but I knew it was the night before he sold the gray colt, and that was the 24th of April.

"'Well,' says Sim Decker, 'on the twenty-third day of April, Ben Dighton was hung to the yard-arm, and I see 'em do it, Lord help him! I did n't mean to tell the women, and I s'posed you'd never know, for I'm all the one of the ship's company you're ever likely to see. We were taken prisoner, and Ben was mad as fire, and they were scared of him and chained him to the deck; and while he was sulking there, a little parrot of a midshipman come up and grinned at him and snapped his fingers in his face; and Ben lifted his hands with the heavy irons and sprung at him like a tiger, and the boy dropped dead as a stone; and they put the bight of a rope round Ben's neck and slung him right up to the yard-arm, and there he swung back and forth until, as soon as we dared, one of us clim' up and cut the rope and let him go over the ship's side; and they put us in irons for that, curse 'em! How did that old man in there know, and he bedridden here, nigh upon three thousand miles off?' says he. But I guess there was n't any of us could tell him," said Captain Lant in conclusion. "It 's something I never could account for, but it 's true as truth. I 've known more such cases; some folks laughs at me for believing 'em, — 'the cap'n's yarns,' they calls 'em, — but if you 'll notice, everybody 's got some yarn of that kind they do believe, if they won't believe yours. And there 's a good deal happens in the world that 's myster'ous. Now there was Widder Oliver Pinkham, over to the P'int, told me with her own lips that she" — But just here we saw the captain's expression alter suddenly, and looked around to see a wagon coming up the lane. We immediately said we must go home, for it was growing late, but asked permission to come again and hear the Widow Oliver Pinkham story. We stopped, however, to see "the women-folks," and afterward became so intimate with them that we were invited to spend the afternoon and take tea, which invitation we accepted with great pride. We went out fishing, also, with the captain and "Danny," of whom I will tell you presently. I often think of Captain Lant in the winter, for he told Kate once that he "felt master old in winter to what he did in summer." He likes reading, fortunately, and we had a letter from him, not long ago, acknowledging the receipt of some books of travel by land and water which we had luckily thought to send him. He gave the latitude and longitude of Deephaven at the beginning of his letter, and signed himself, "Respectfully yours with esteem, Jacob Lant (condemned as unseaworthy)."

Danny

DEEPHAVEN seemed more like one of the lazy little English seaside towns than any other. It was not in the least American. There was no excitement about anything; there were no manufactories; nobody seemed in the least hurry. The only foreigners were a few stranded sailors. I do not know when a house or a new building of any kind had been built; the men were farmers, or went outward in boats, or inward in fish-wagons, or sometimes mackerel and halibut fishing in schooners for the city markets. Sometimes a schooner came to one of the wharves to load with hay or firewood;

but Deephaven used to be a town of note, rich and busy, as its forsaken warehouses show.

We knew almost all the fisherpeople at the shore, even old Dinnett, who lived an apparently desolate life by himself in a tumble-down hut and was reputed to have been a bloodthirsty pirate in his youth. He was consequently feared by all the children, and for misdemeanors in his latter days avoided generally. Kate talked with him awhile one day on the shore, and made him come up with her for a bandage for his hand which she saw he had hurt badly; and the next morning he brought us a "new" lobster apiece, — fishermen mean that a thing is only not salted when they say it is "fresh." We happened to be in the hall, and received him ourselves, and gave him a great piece of tobacco and (unintentionally) the means of drinking our health. "Bless your pretty hearts!" said he; "may ye be happy, and live long, and get good husbands, and if they ain't good to you may they die from you!"

None of our friends were more interesting than the fishermen. The fish-houses, which might be called the business centre of the town, were at a little distance from the old warehouses, farther down the harbor shore, and were ready to fall down in despair. There were some fishermen who lived near by, but most of them were also farmers in a small way, and lived in the village or farther inland. From our eastern windows we could see the moorings, and we always liked to watch the boats go out or come straying in, one after the other, tipping and skimming under the square little sails; and we often went down to the fish-houses to see what kind of a catch there had been.

I should have imagined that the sea would become very commonplace to men whose business was carried on in boats, and who had spent night after night and day after day from their boyhood on the water; but that is a mistake. They have an awe of the sea and of its mysteries, and of what it hides away from us. They are childish in their wonder at any strange creature which they find. If they have not seen the sea-serpent, they believe, I am sure, that other people have; and when a great shark or black-fish or sword-fish was taken and brought in shore, everybody went to see it, and we talked about it, and how brave its conqueror was, and what a fight there had been, for a long time afterward.

I said that we liked to see the boats go

out; but I must not give you the impression that we saw them often, for they weighed anchor at an early hour in the morning. I remember once there was a light fog over the sea, lifting fast, as the sun was coming up, and the brownish sails disappeared in the mist, while voices could still be heard for some minutes after the men were hidden from sight. This gave one a curious feeling, but afterward, when the sun had risen, everything looked much the same as usual; the fog had gone, and the dories and even the larger boats were distant specks on the sparkling sea.

One afternoon we made a new acquaintance in this wise. We went down to the shore to see if we could hire a conveyance to the lighthouse the next morning. We often went out early in one of the fishing-boats; and after we had stayed as long as we pleased, Mr. Kew would bring us home. It was quiet enough that day, for not a single boat had come in, and there were no men to be seen alongshore. There was a solemn company of lobster-coops, or cages, which had been brought in to be mended. They always amused Kate. She said they seemed to her like droll old women telling each other secrets. These were scattered about in different attitudes, and looked more confidential than usual.

Just as we were going away, we happened to see a man at work in one of the sheds. He was the fisherman whom we knew least of all; an odd-looking, silent sort of man, more sunburnt and weatherbeaten than any of the others. We had learned to know him by the bright red flannel shirt he always wore, and besides, he was lame; some one told us he had had a bad fall once, on board ship. Kate and I had always wished we could find a chance to talk with him. He looked up at us pleasantly; and when we nodded and smiled, he said "Good day" in a gruff, hearty voice, and went on with his work, cleaning mackerel.

"Do you mind our watching you?" asked Kate.

"No, *ma'am!*" said the fisherman emphatically. So there we stood.

Those fish-houses were curious places, so different from any other kind of workshop. In this there was a seine, or part of one, festooned among the cross-beams overhead, and there were snarled fishing-lines, and barrows to carry fish in, like wheelbarrows without wheels; there were the queer round lobster-nets, and "kits" of salt mackerel, tubs of bait, and piles of clams; and some queer bones, and parts of remarkable fish, and lobster-claws of surprising size fastened on the walls for ornament. There was a pile of rubbish down at the end; I dare say it was all useful, however, — there is such mystery about the business.

Kate and I were never tired of hearing of the fish that come at different times of the year, and go away again, like the birds; or of the actions of the dog-fish, which the 'longshoremen hate so bitterly; and then there are such curious legends and traditions, of which almost all fishermen have a store.

"I think mackerel are the prettiest fish that swim," said I presently.

"So do I," said the man, "not to say but I 've seen more fancy-looking fish down in southern waters, bright as any flower you ever see; but a mackerel," holding up one admiringly, "why, they 're so clean-built and trig-looking! Put a cod alongside, and he looks as lumbering as an old-fashioned Dutch brig aside a yacht.

"Those are good-looking fish, but they an't made much account of," continued our friend, as he pushed aside the mackerel and took another tub. "They 're hake, I s'pose you know. But I forgot, — I can't stop to bother with them now." And he pulled forward a barrow full of small fish, flat and hard, with pointed, bony heads.

The Fish Houses

"Those are porgies, aren't they?" asked Kate.

"Yes," said the man, "an' I'm going to sliver them for the trawls."

We knew what the trawls were, and supposed that the porgies were to be used for bait; and we soon found out what "slivering" meant, by seeing him take them by the head and cut a slice from first one side and then the other in such a way that the pieces looked not unlike smaller fish.

"It seems to me," said I, "that fishermen always have sharper knives than other people."

"Yes, we do like a sharp knife in our trade; and then we are mostly strong-handed."

He was throwing the porgies' heads and backbones — all that was left of them after slivering — in a heap; and now several cats walked in as if they felt at home, and began a hearty lunch. "What a troop of pussies there is round here," said I; "I wonder what will become of them in the winter, — though, to be sure, the fishing goes on just the same."

"The better part of them don't get through the cold weather," said Danny. "Two or three of the old ones have been here for some years, and are as much belonging to Deephaven as the meetin'-house; but the rest of them an't to be depended on. You'll miss the young ones by the dozen, come spring. I don't know myself but they move inland in the fall of the year; they're knowing enough, if that's all!"

Kate and I stood in the wide doorway, arm in arm, looking sometimes at the queer fisherman and the porgies, and sometimes out to sea. It was low tide; the wind had risen a little, and the heavy salt air blew toward us from the wet brown ledges in the rocky harbor. The sea was bright blue, and the sun was shining. Two gulls were swinging lazily to and fro; there was a flock of sandpipers down by the water's edge, in a great hurry, as usual.

Presently the fisherman spoke again, beginning with an odd laugh: "I *was* scared last winter! Jack Scudder and me, we were up in the Cap'n Manning storehouse hunting for a half-bar'l of salt the skipper said was there. It was an awful blustering kind of day, with a thin icy rain blowing from all points at once; sea roaring as if it wished it could come ashore and put a stop to everything. Bad days at sea, them are; rigging all froze up. As I was saying, we were hunting for a half-bar'l of salt, and I laid hold of a bar'l that had something heavy in the bottom, and tilted it up, and my eye! there was a stir and a scratch and a squeal, and out went some kind of a creatur', and I jumped back, not looking for anything live, but I see in a minute it was a cat; and perhaps you think it is a big story, but there were eight more in there, hived in together to keep warm. I car'd 'em up some new fish that night; they seemed short of provisions. We had n't been out fishing as much as common, and they had n't dared to be round the fish-houses much, for a fellow who came in on a coaster had a dog, and he used to chase 'em. Hard chance they had, and lots of 'em died, I guess; but there seem to be some survivin' relatives, an' al'ays just so hungry! I used to feed them some when I was ashore. I think likely you 've heard that a cat will fetch you bad luck; but I don't know 's that made much difference to me. I kind of like to keep on the right side of 'em, too; if ever I have a bad dream there 's sure to be a cat in it; but I was brought up to be clever to dumb beasts, an' I guess it 's my natur'. Except fish," said Danny, after a minute's thought; "but then it never seems like they had feelin's like creatur's that live ashore." And we all laughed heartily and felt well acquainted.

"I s'pose you ladies will laugh if I tell ye I kept a kitty once myself." This was said rather shyly, and there was evidently a story, so we were much interested, and Kate said, "Please tell us about it; was it at sea?"

"Yes, it was at sea; leastways, on a coaster. I got her in a sing'lar kind of way: it was one afternoon we were lying alongside Charlestown Bridge, and I heard a young cat screeching real pitiful; and after I looked all round, I see her in the water clutching on to the pier of the bridge, and some little divils of boys were heaving rocks down at her. I got into the schooner's tag-boat quick, I tell ye, and pushed off for her, 'n' she let go just as I got there, 'n' I guess you never saw a more miser'ble-looking creatur' than I fished out of the water. Cold weather it was. Her leg was hurt, and her eye, and I thought first I 'd drop her overboard again, and then I did n't, and I took her aboard the schooner and put her by the stove. I thought she might as well die where it was warm. She eat a little mite of chowder before night, but she was very slim; but next morning, when I went to see if she was dead, she fell to licking my finger, and she did purr away

Danny

like a dolphin. One of her eyes was out, where a stone had took her, and she never got any use of it; but she used to look at you so clever with the other, and she got well of her lame foot after a while. I got to be ter'ble fond of her. She was just the knowingest thing you ever saw, and she used to sleep alongside of me in my bunk, and like as not she would go on deck with me when it was my watch. I was coasting then most o' the time for a year and eight months, and I kept her long of me. We used to be in harbor consider'ble, and about eight o'clock in the forenoon I used to drop a line and catch her a couple of cunners. Now, it is cur'us that she used to know when I was fishing for her. She would pounce on them fish and carry 'em off and growl, and she knew when I got a bite, — she 'd watch the line; but when we were mackereling she never give us any trouble. She would never lift a paw to touch any of our fish. She did n't have the thieving ways common to most cats. She used to set round on deck in fair weather, but when the wind blew she al'ays kept herself below. Sometimes when we were in port she would go ashore a while, and fetch back a bird or a mouse, but she would n't never eat it till she come and showed it to me. She never wanted to stop long ashore, though I did n't shut her up; I always give her her liberty. I got a good deal of joking about her from the fellows, but she was a sight of company. I don' know as I ever had anything like me as much as she did. Not to say as I ever had much of any trouble with anybody, ashore or afloat. But then, I han't had a home, what I call a home, since I was going on nine year old."

"How has that happened?" asked Kate.

"Well, mother, she died, and I was bound out to a man in the tanning trade, and I hated him, and I hated the trade; and when I was a little bigger I ran away, and I 've followed the sea ever since. I was n't much use to him, I guess; leastways, he never took the trouble to hunt me up.

"About the best place I ever was in was a hospital. It was in foreign parts. Ye see I 'm crippled some? I fell from the topsail yard to the deck, and I struck my shoulder, and broke my leg, and banged myself all up. It was to a nuns' hospital where they took me. All of the nuns were Catholics, and they wore white things on their heads. I don't suppose you ever saw any. Have you? Well, now, that 's queer! When I was first there I was scared of them; they were real ladies, and I was n't used to being in a house, any way. One of them, that took care of me most of the time, why, she would even set up half the night with me, and I could n't begin to tell you how good-natured she was, an' she 'd look real sorry, too. I used to be ugly, I ached so, along in the first of my being there, but I spoke of it when I was coming away, and she said it was all right. She used to feed me, that lady did; and there were some days I could n't lift my head, and she would rise it on her arm. She give me a little mite of a book when I come away. I 'm not much of a hand at reading, but I always kept it on account of her. She was so pleased when I got so 's to set up in a chair and look out of the window. She was n't much of a hand to talk English. I did feel bad to come away from there; I 'most wished I could be sick a while longer. I never said much of anything either, and I don't know but she thought it was queer; but I am a dreadful clumsy man to say anything, and I got flustered. I don't know 's I mind telling you; I was 'most a-crying. I used to think I 'd lay by some money and ship for there and carry her something real pretty. But I don't rank able-bodied seaman like I used, and it 's as much as I can do to get a berth on a coaster; I suppose I might go as cook. I liked to have died with my hurt at that hospital; but when I was getting well it made me think of when I was a mite of a chap to home before mother died, to be laying there in a clean bed with somebody to do for me. Guess you think I 'm a good hand to talk; somehow it comes easy to-day."

"What became of your cat?" asked Kate, after a pause, during which our friend sliced away at the porgies.

"I never rightly knew; it was in Salem harbor and a windy night. I was on deck consider'ble, for the schooner pitched lively, and once or twice she dragged her anchor. I never saw the kitty after she eat her supper. I remember I gave her some milk, — I used to buy her a pint once in a while for a treat; I don't know but she might have gone off on a cake of ice, but it did seem as if she had too much sense for that. Most likely she missed her footing, and fell overboard in the dark. She was marked real pretty, black and white, and kep' herself just as clean! She knew as well as could be when foul weather was coming; she would bother round and act queer; but when the sun was out she would sit round on deck as pleased as a queen. There! I feel bad sometimes when I think of her, and I never went into Salem since without hoping that I should see her. I don't know but if I was a-going to begin my life over again, I 'd settle down ashore and have a snug little house and farm it. But I guess I shall do better at fishing. Give me a trig-built topsail schooner painted up nice, with a stripe on her, and clean sails, and a fresh wind with the sun a-shining, and I feel first-rate."

"Do you believe that codfish swallow stones before a storm?" asked Kate. I had been thinking about the lonely fisherman in a sentimental way, and so irrelevant a question shocked me. "I saw he felt slightly embarrassed at having talked about his affairs so much," Kate told me afterward, "and I thought we should leave him feeling more at his ease if we talked about fish for a while." And sure enough he did seem relieved, and gave us his opinion about the codfish at once, adding that he never cared much for cod any way; folks up country bought 'em a good deal, he heard. Give him a haddock right out of the water for his dinner!

"I never can remember," said Kate, "whether it is cod or haddock that have a black stripe along their sides" —

"Oh, those are haddock," said I; "they say that the devil caught a haddock once, and it slipped through his fingers and got scorched, so all the haddock had the same mark afterward."

"Well, now, how did you know that old story?" said Danny, laughing heartily; "ye must n't believe all the old stories ye hear, mind ye!"

"Oh, no," said we.

"Hullo! There 's Jim Toggerson's boat close in shore. She sets low in the water, so he 's done well. He and Skipper Scudder have been out deep-sea fishing since yesterday."

Our friend pushed the porgies back into a corner, stuck his knife into a beam, and we hurried down to the shore. Kate and I sat on the pebbles, and he went out to the moorings in a dirty dory to help unload the fish.

We afterward saw a great deal of Danny, as all the men called him. But though Kate and I tried our best and used our utmost skill and tact to make him tell us more about himself, he never did. But perhaps there was nothing more to be told.

The day we left Deephaven we went down to the shore to say good-by to him and to some other friends, and he said, "Goin', are ye? Well, I 'm sorry; ye 've treated me first-rate; the Lord bless ye!" and then was so much mortified at the way he had said farewell that he turned and fled round the corner of the fish-house.

Captain Sands

OLD Captain Sands was one of the most prominent citizens of Deephaven, and a very good friend of Kate's and mine. We often met him, and grew much interested in him before we knew him well. He had a reputation in town for being peculiar and somewhat visionary ; but every one seemed to like him, and at last one morning, when we happened to be on our way to the wharves, we stopped at the door of an old warehouse, which we had never seen opened before. Captain Sands sat just inside, smoking his pipe, and we said good morning, and asked him if he did not think there was a fog coming in by and by. We had thought a little of going out to the lighthouse. The cap'n rose slowly, and came out so that he could see farther round to the east. "There's some scud coming in a'ready," said he. "None to speak of yet, I don't know's you can see it, — yes, yes, you're right; there's a heavy bank of fog lyin' off, but it won't be in under two or three hours yet, unless the wind backs round more and freshens up. Were n't thinking of going out, were ye?"

"A little," said Kate, "but we had nearly given it up. We are getting to be very weather-wise, and we pride ourselves on being quick at seeing fogs." At which the cap'n smiled and said we were consider'ble young to know much about weather, but it looked well that we took some interest in it; most young people were fools about weather, and would just as soon set off to go anywhere right under the edge of a thunder-shower. "Come in and set down, won't ye?" he added; "it ain't much of a place; I've got a lot of old stuff stowed away here that the women-folks don't want up to the house. I'm a great hand for keeping things." And he looked round fondly at the contents of the low room. "I come down here once in a while and let in the sun, and sometimes I want to hunt up something or 'nother; kind of stow-away place, ye see." And then he laughed apologetically, rubbing his hands together, and looking out to sea again as if he wished to appear unconcerned; yet we saw that he wondered if we thought it ridiculous for a man of his age to have treasured up so much trumpery in that cobwebby place. There were some whole oars and the sail of his boat and two or three killicks and painters, not to forget a heap of wornout oars and sails in one corner and a sailor's hammock slung across the beam overhead, and there were some sailor's chests and the capstan of a ship and innumerable boxes which all seemed to be stuffed full, besides no end of things lying on the floor and packed away on shelves and hanging to rusty big-headed nails in the wall. I saw some great lumps of coral, and large, rough shells, a great hornet's nest, and a monstrous lobster-shell. The cap'n had cobbled and tied up some remarkable old chairs for the accommodation of himself and his friends.

"What a nice place!" said Kate in a frank, delighted way which could not have failed to be gratifying.

"Well, no," said the cap'n, with his slow smile, "it ain't what you 'd rightly call 'nice,' as I know of: it ain't never been cleared out all at once since I began putting in. There 's nothing that 's worth anything, either, to anybody but me. Wife, she 's said to me a hundred times, 'Why don't you overhaul them old things and burn 'em?' She 's al'ays at me about letting the property, as if it were a corner-lot in Broadway. That 's all women-folks know about business!" And here the captain caught himself tripping, and looked uneasy for a minute. "I suppose I might have let it for a fish-house, but it 's most too far from the shore to be handy — and — well — there are some things here that I set a good deal by."

"Is n't that a sword-fish's sword in that piece of wood?" Kate asked, presently; and was answered that it was found broken off as we saw it, in the hull of a wreck that went ashore on Blue P'int when the captain was a young man, and he had sawed it out and kept it ever since, — fifty-nine years. Of course we went closer to look at it, and we both felt a great sympathy for this friend of ours, because we have the same fashion of keeping worthless treasures, and we understood perfectly how dear such things may be.

"Do you mind if we look round a little?" I asked, doubtfully, for I knew how I should hate having strangers look over my own treasury. But Captain Sands looked pleased at our interest, and said cheerfully that we might overhaul as much as we chose. Kate discovered first an old battered wooden figure-head of a ship, — a woman's head with long curly hair falling over the shoulders. The paint was almost gone, and the dust covered most of what was left: still there was a wonderful spirit and grace, and a wild, weird beauty which attracted us exceedingly; but the captain could only tell us that it had belonged to the wreck of a Danish brig which had been driven on the reef where the lighthouse stands now, and his father had found this on the long sands a day or two afterward. "That was a dreadful storm," said the captain. "I 've heard the old folks tell about it; it was when I was only a year or two old. There were three merchantmen wrecked within five miles of Deephaven. This one was all stove to splinters, and they used to say she had treasure aboard. When I was small I used to have a great idea of going out there to the rocks at low water and trying to find some gold, but I never made out no great." And he smiled indulgently at the thought of his youthful dream.

"Kate," said I, "do you see what beauties these Turk's-head knots are?" We had

Captain Sands

been taking a course of first lessons in knots from Danny, and had followed by learning some charmingly intricate ones from Captain Lant, the stranded mariner who lived on a farm two miles or so inland. Kate came over to look at the Turk's-heads, which were at either end of the rope handle of a little dark-blue chest.

Captain Sands turned in his chair and nodded approval. "That 's a neat piece of work, and it was a first-rate seaman who did it; he 's dead and gone years ago, poor young fellow; an I-talian he was, who sailed on the Ranger three or four long voyages. He fell from the mast-head on the voyage home from Callao. Cap'n Manning and old Mr. Lorimer, they owned the Ranger, and when she come into port and they got the news, they took it as much to heart as if he 'd been some relation. He was smart as a whip, and had a way with him, and the pleasantest kind of a voice; you could n't help liking him. They found out that he had a mother alive in Port Mahon, and they sent his pay and some money he had in the bank at Riverport out to her by a ship that was going to the Mediterranean. He had some clothes in his chest, and they sold those and sent her the money, — all but some trinkets they supposed he was keeping for her; I rec'lect he used to speak consider'ble about his mother. I shipped one v'y'ge with him before the mast, before I went out mate of the Daylight. I happened to be in port the time the Ranger got in, an' I see this chist lying round in Cap'n Manning's storehouse, and I offered to give him what it was worth; but we was good friends, and he told me to take it if I wanted it, it was no use to him, and I 've kept it ever since.

"There are some of his traps in it now, I believe; ye can look." And we took off some tangled cod-lines and opened the chest. There was only a round wooden box in the till, and in some idle hour at sea the young sailor had carved his initials and an anchor and the date on the cover. We found some sail-needles and a palm in this "ditty-box," as the sailors call it, and a little string of buttons with some needles and yarn and thread in a neat little bag, which perhaps his mother had made for him when he started off on his first voyage. Besides these things there was only a fanciful little broken buckle, green and gilt, which he might have picked up in some foreign street, and his protection-paper carefully folded, wherein he was certified as being a citizen of the United States, with dark complexion and dark hair.

"He was one of the pleasantest fellows that ever I shipped with," said the captain, with a gruff tenderness in his voice. "Always willin' to do his work himself, and like 's not when the other fellows up the rigging were cold, or ugly about something or 'nother, he 'd say something that would set them all laughing, and somehow it made you good-natured to see him round. He was brought up a Catholic, I s'pose; anyway, he had some beads, and sometimes they would joke him about 'em on board ship, but he would blaze up in a minute, ugly as a tiger. I never saw him mad about anything else, though he would n't stand it if anybody tried to crowd him. He fell from the main-to'-gallant yard to the deck, and was dead when they picked him up. They were off the Bermudas. I suppose he lost his balance, but I never could see how; he was sure-footed, and as quick as a cat. They said they saw him try to catch at the stay, but there was a heavy sea running, and the ship rolled just so 's to let him through between the rigging, and he struck the deck like a stone. I don't know 's that chest has been opened these ten years, — I declare it carries me back to look at those poor little traps of his. Well, it 's the way of the world; we think we 're somebody, and we have our day, but it is n't long afore we 're forgotten."

The captain reached over for the paper, and, taking out a clumsy pair of steel-bowed spectacles, read it through carefully. "I 'll warrant he took good care of this," said he. "He was an I-talian, and no more of an American citizen than a Chinese; I wonder he had n't called himself John Jones, that 's the name most of the foreigners used to take when they got their papers. I remember once I was sick with a fever in Chelsea Hospital, and one morning they came bringing in the mate of a Portugee brig on a stretcher, and the surgeon asked what his name was. 'John Jones,' says he. 'Oh, say something else,' says the surgeon; 'we 've got five John Joneses here a'ready, and it 's getting to be no name at all.' Sailors are great hands for false names; they have a trick of using them when they have any money to leave ashore, for fear their shipmates will go and draw it out. I suppose there are thousands of dollars unclaimed in New York banks, where men have left it charged to their false names; then they get lost at sea or something, and never go to get it, and nobody knows whose it is. They 're curious folks, take 'em altogether, sailors is; specially these foreign fellows that wander about from ship to ship. They 're getting to be a dreadful low set, too, of late years. It 's the last thing I 'd want a boy of mine to do, — ship before the mast with one of these mixed crews. It 's a dog's life, anyway, and the risks and the chances against you are awful. It 's a good while before you can lay up anything, unless you are part owner. I saw all the p'ints a good deal plainer after I quit followin' the sea myself, though I 've always been more or less into navigation until this last war come on. I know when I was ship's husband of the Polly and Susan, there was a young man went out cap'n of her, — her last voyage, and she never was heard from. He had a wife and two or three little children ; and for all he was so smart, they would have been about the same as beggars, if I had n't happened to have his life insured the day I was having the papers made out for the ship. I happened to think of it. Five thousand dollars there was, and I sent it to the widow along with his primage. She had n't expected nothing, or next to nothing, and she was pleased, I tell ye."

"I think it was very kind in you to think of that, Captain Sands," said Kate. And the old man said, flushing a little, "Well, I 'm not so smart as some of the men who started when I did, and some of 'em went ahead of me, but some of 'em did n't, after all. I 've tried to be honest, and to do just about as nigh right as I could, and you know there 's an old sayin' that a cripple in the right road will beat a racer in the wrong."

The Circus at Denby

KATE and I looked forward to a certain Saturday with as much eagerness as if we had been little school-boys, for on that day we were to go to a circus at Denby, a town perhaps eight miles inland. There had not been a circus so near Deephaven for a long time, and nobody had dared to believe the first rumor of it, until two dashing young men had deigned to come themselves to put up the big posters on the end of 'Bijah Mauley's barn. All the boys in town came as soon as possible to see these amazing pictures, and some were wretched in their secret hearts at the thought that they might not see the show itself. Tommy Dockum was more interested than any one else, and mentioned the subject so frequently one day, when he went raspberrying with us, that we grew enthusiastic, and told each other what fun it would be to go, for everybody would be there, and it would be the greatest loss to us if we were absent. I thought I had lost my childish fondness for circuses, but it came back redoubled; and Kate may contradict me if she chooses, but I am sure she never looked forward to an Easter Oratorio with half the pleasure she did to this "caravan," as most of the people called it.

We felt that it was a great pity that any of the boys and girls should be left lamenting at home; and finding that there were some of our acquaintances and Tommy's who saw no chance of going, we engaged Jo Sands and Leander Dockum to carry them to Denby in two fish-wagons, with boards laid across for the extra seats. We saw them join the straggling train of carriages which had begun to go through the village from all along shore, soon after daylight, and they started on their journey shouting and carousing, with their pockets crammed with early apples and other provisions. We thought it would have been fun enough to see the people go by, for we had had no idea until then how many inhabitants that country held.

We had asked Mrs. Kew to go with us;

but she was half an hour later than she had promised, for, since there was no wind, she could not come ashore in the sail-boat, and Mr. Kew had to row her in in the dory. We saw the boat at last nearly in shore, and drove down to meet it: even the horse seemed to realize what a great day it was, and showed a disposition to friskiness, evidently as surprising to himself as to us.

Mrs. Kew was funnier that day than we had ever known her, which is saying a great deal, and we should not have had half so good a time if she had not been with us; although she lived in the lighthouse, and had no chance to "see passing," which a woman prizes so highly in the country, she had a wonderful memory for faces, and could tell us the names of all Deephaveners and of most of the people we met outside its limits. She looked impressive and solemn as she hurried up from the water's edge, giving Mr. Kew some parting charges over her shoulder as he pushed off the boat to go back; but after we had convinced her that the delay had not troubled us, she seemed more cheerful. It was evident that she felt the importance of the occasion, and that she was pleased at our having chosen her for company. She threw back her veil entirely, sat very straight, and took immense pains to bow to every acquaintance whom she met. She wore her best Sunday clothes, and her manner was formal for the first few minutes; it was evident that she felt we were meeting under unusual circumstances, and that, although we had often met before on the friendliest terms, our having asked her to make this excursion in public required a different sort of behavior at her hands, and a due amount of ceremony and propriety. But this state of things did not last long, as she soon made a remark at which Kate and I laughed so heartily, in lighthouse-acquaintance fashion, that she unbent, and gave her whole mind to enjoying herself.

When we came by the store where the post-office was kept, we saw a small knot of people gathered round the door, and stopped to see what had happened. There was a forlorn horse standing near, with his harness tied up with fuzzy ends of rope, and the wagon was cobbled together with pieces of board; the whole craft looked as if it might be wrecked with the least jar. In the wagon were four or five stupid-looking boys and girls, one of whom was crying softly. Their father was ill, some one told us. "He was took faint, but he is coming to all right; they have give him something to take: their name

Posters on 'Bijah Mauley's Barn

is Craper, and they live way over beyond the Ridge, on Stone Hill. They were goin' over to Denby to the circus, and the man was calc'lating to get doctored, but I d' know 's he can get so fur; he 's powerful slim-looking to me." Kate and I went to see if we could be of any use; and when we went into the store we saw the man leaning back in his chair, looking ghastly pale, and as if he were far gone in consumption. Kate spoke to him, and he said he was better; he had felt bad all the way along, but he had n't given in. He was pitiful, poor fellow, with his evident attempt at dressing up. He had the bushiest, dustiest red hair and whiskers, which made the pallor of his face still more striking, and his illness had thinned and paled his rough, clumsy hands. I thought what a hard piece of work it must have been for him to start for the circus that morning, and how kind-hearted he must be to have made such an effort for his children's pleasure. As we went out they stared at us gloomily. The shadow of their disappointment touched and chilled our pleasure.

Somebody had turned the horse so that he was heading toward home, and by his actions he showed that he was the only one of the party who was glad. We were so sorry for the children; perhaps it had promised to be the happiest day of their lives, and now they must go back to their uninteresting home without having seen the great show.

"I am so sorry you are disappointed," said Kate, as we were wondering how the man who had followed us could ever climb into the wagon.

"Heh?" said he, blankly, as if he did not know what her words meant. "What fool has been a-turning o' this horse?" he asked a man who was looking on.

"Why, which way be ye goin'?"

"To the circus," said Mr. Craper, with decision; "where d' ye s'pose? That 's where I started for, anyways." And he climbed in and glanced round to count the children, struck the horse with the willow switch, and they started off briskly, while everybody laughed. Kate and I joined Mrs. Kew, who had enjoyed the scene.

"Well, there!" said she, "I wonder the folks in the old North burying-ground ain't a-rising up to go to Denby to that caravan!"

We reached Denby at noon; it was an uninteresting town which had grown up about some mills. There was a great commotion in the streets, and it was evident that we had lost much in not having seen the procession.

There was a great deal of business going on in the shops, and there were two or three hand-organs at large, near one of which we stopped awhile to listen, just after we had met Leander and given the horse into his charge. Mrs. Kew finished her shopping as soon as possible, and we hurried toward the great tents, where all the flags were flying. I think I have not told you that we were to have the benefit of seeing a menagerie in addition to the circus, and you may be sure we went faithfully round to see everything that the cages held.

I cannot truthfully say that it was a good show; it was somewhat dreary, now that I think of it quietly and without excitement. The creatures looked tired, and as if they had been on the road for a great many years. The animals were all old, and there was a shabby great elephant whose look of general discouragement went to my heart, for it seemed as if he were miserably conscious of a misspent life. He stood dejected and motionless at one side of the tent, and it was hard to believe that there was a spark of vitality left in him. A great number of the people had never seen an elephant before, and we heard a thin little old man, who stood near us, say delightedly, "There 's the old creatur', and no mistake, Ann 'Liza. I wanted to see him most of anything. My sakes alive, ain't he big!"

And Ann 'Liza, who was stout and sleepy-looking, droned out, "Ye-es, there 's consider'ble of him ; but he looks as if he hain't got no sprawl."

Kate and I turned away and laughed, while Mrs. Kew said confidentially, as the couple moved away, "*She* need n't be a-reflectin' on the poor beast. That 's Mis' Seth Tanner, and there is n't a woman in Deephaven nor East Parish to be named the same day with her for laziness. I 'm glad she did n't catch sight of me; she 'd have talked about nothing for a fortnight."

There was a picture of a huge snake in Deephaven, and I was just wondering where he could be, or if there ever had been one, when we heard a boy ask the same question of the man whose thankless task it was to stir up the lions with a stick to make them roar. "The snake 's dead," he answered good-naturedly. "Did n't you have to dig an awful long grave for him?" asked the boy; but the man said he reckoned they curled him up some, and smiled as he turned to his lions, who looked as if they needed a tonic. Everybody lingered longest before

"My sakes alive, ain't he big!"

the monkeys, who seemed to be the only lively creatures in the whole collection; and finally we made our way into the other tent, and perched ourselves on a high seat, from whence we had a capital view of the audience and the ring, and could see the people come in. Mrs. Kew was on the lookout for acquaintances, and her spirits as well as our own seemed to rise higher and higher. She was on the alert, moving her head this way and that to catch sight of people, giving us a running commentary in the mean time. It was very pleasant to see a person so happy as Mrs. Kew was that day, and I dare say in speaking of the occasion she would say the same thing of Kate and me, — for it was such a good time! We bought some peanuts, without which no circus seems complete, and we listened to the conversations which were being carried on round us while we were waiting for the performance to begin. There were two old farmers whom we had noticed occasionally in Deephaven; one was telling the other, with great confusion of pronouns, about a big pig which had lately been killed. "John did feel dreadful disappointed at having to kill now," we heard him say, "bein' as he had calc'lated to kill along near Thanksgivin' time; there was goin' to be a new moon then, and he expected to get seventy-five or a hundred pound more on to him. But he did n't seem to gain, and me and 'Bijah both told him he'd do better to kill now, while everything was favor'ble, and if he set out to wait, something might happen to him; and then I've always held that you can't get no hog only just so fur; for my part I don't like these great overgrown creatur's. I like well enough to see a hog that'll weigh six hunderd, just for the beauty on't, but for my eatin' give me one that'll just rise three. 'Bijah's accurate, and says he is goin' to weigh risin' five hundred and fifty. I shall stop, as I go home, to John's wife's brother's and see if they've got the particulars yet; John was goin' to get the scales this morning. I guess likely consider'ble many'll gather there tomorrow after meeting. John did n't calc'late to cut up till Monday."

"I guess likely I'll stop in to-morrow," said the other man; "I like to see a han'some hog. Chester white, you said? Consider them best, don't ye?" But this question never was answered, for the greater part of the circus company in gorgeous trappings came parading in.

The circus was like all other circuses, except that it was shabbier than most, and the performers seemed to have less heart in it than usual. They did their best, and went through with their parts conscientiously, but they looked as if they never had had a good time in their lives. The audience was hilarious, and cheered and laughed at the tired clown until he looked as if he thought his speeches might possibly be funny, after all. We were so glad we had pleased the poor thing; and when he sang a song our satisfaction was still greater, and so he sang it all over again. Perhaps he had been associating with people who were used to circuses. The afternoon was hot, and the boys with Japanese fans and trays of lemonade did a remarkable business for so late in the season; the brass band on the other side of the tent shrieked its very best, and all the young men of the region had brought their girls; and some of these countless pairs of country lovers we watched a great deal, as they "kept company" with more or less depth of satisfaction in each other. We had a grand chance to see the fashions, and there were many old people and a great number of little children, and some families had evidently locked their house door behind them, since they had brought both the dog and the baby.

"Does n't it seem as if you were a child again?" Kate asked me. "I am sure this is just the same as the first circus I ever saw. It grows more and more familiar, and it puzzles me to think they should not have altered in the least while I have changed so much, and have even had time to grow up. You don't know how it is making me remember other things of which I have not thought for years. I was seven years old when I went that first time. Uncle Jack invited me. I had a new parasol, and he laughed because I would hold it over my shoulder when the sun was in my face. He took me into the side-shows, and bought me everything I asked for on the way home, and we did not get home until twilight. The rest of the family had dined at five o'clock and gone out for a long drive, and it was such fun to have our dinner by ourselves. I sat at the head of the table in mamma's place; and when Bridget came down and insisted that I must go to bed, Uncle Jack came softly up stairs and sat by the window, smoking and telling me stories. He ran and hid in the closet when we heard mamma coming up, and when she found him out by the cigar-smoke and made believe scold him, I thought she was in earnest, and begged him off. Yes; and I remember that

Bridget sat in the next room, making her new dress so she could wear it to church, next day. I thought it was a beautiful dress, and besought mamma to have one like it. It was bright green with yellow spots all over it," said Kate. "Ah, poor Uncle Jack! he was so good to me! We were always telling stories of what we would do when I was grown up and he came home from China. He died in Canton the next year, and I cried myself ill; but for a long time I thought he might not be dead, after all, and might come home any day. He used to seem so old to me, and he really was just out of college and not so old as I am now. That day at the circus he had a pink rosebud in his buttonhole, and — oh! when have I ever thought of this before! — a woman sat before us who had a stiff little cape on her bonnet like a shelf, and I carefully put peanuts round the edge of it, and when she moved her head they would fall. I thought it was the best fun in the world, and I wished Uncle Jack to ride the donkey; I was sure he could keep on, because his horse had capered about with him one day on Beacon Street, and I thought him a perfect rider, since nothing had happened to him then."

"I remember," said Mrs. Kew presently,

"that just before I was married 'he' took me over to Wareham Corners to a caravan. My sister Hannah and the young man who was keeping company with her went too. I have n't been to one since till to-day, and it does carry me back same 's it does you, Miss Kate. It does n't seem more than five years ago, and what would I have thought if I had known 'he' and I were going to keep a lighthouse and be contented there, what 's more, and sometimes not get ashore for a fortnight; settled, gray-headed old folks! We were gay enough in those days. I know old Miss Sabrina Smith warned me that I 'd better think twice before I took up with Tom Kew, for he was a light-minded young man. I speak o' that to him in the winter-time, when he sets reading the almanac half asleep, and I 'm knitting, and the wind 's a-howling, and the waves coming ashore on those rocks as if they wished they could put out the light and blow down the lighthouse. We were reflected on a good deal for going to that caravan; some of the old folks did n't think it was improvin'— Well, I should think that man was a-trying to break his neck!"

Coming out of the great tent was disagreeable enough, and we seemed to have chosen the worst time, for the crowd pushed fiercely, though I suppose nobody was in the least hurry, and we were all severely jammed, while from somewhere underneath came the wails of a deserted dog. We had not meant to see the side-shows, and went carelessly past two or three tents; but when we came in sight of the picture of the Kentucky giantess, we noticed that Mrs. Kew looked at it wistfully, and we immediately asked if she cared anything about going to see the wonder, whereupon she confessed that she never heard of such a thing as a woman's weighing six hundred and fifty pounds, so we all three went in. There were only two or three persons inside the tent, beside a little boy who played the hand-organ.

The Kentucky giantess sat in two chairs on a platform, and there was a large cage of monkeys just beyond, toward which Kate and I went at once. "Why, she is n't more than two thirds as big the picture," said Mrs. Kew in a regretful whisper; "but I guess she 's big enough; does n't she look discouraged, poor creatur'?" Kate and I felt ashamed of ourselves for being there. No matter if she had consented to be carried round for a show, it must have been horrible to be stared at and joked about day after day; and we gravely looked at the monkeys, and in a few minutes turned to see if Mrs. Kew were not ready to come away, when to our surprise we saw that she was talking to the giantess with great interest, and we went nearer.

"I thought your face looked natural the minute I set foot inside the door," said Mrs. Kew; "but you 've — altered some since I saw you, and I could n't place you till I heard you speak. Why, you used to be spare; I am amazed, Marilly! Where are your folks?"

"I don't wonder you are surprised," said the giantess. "I was a good ways from this when you knew me, was n't I? But father, he run through with every cent he had before he died, and 'he' took to drink, and it killed him after a while, and then I begun to grow worse and worse, till I could n't do nothing to earn a dollar, and everybody was a-coming to see me, till at last I used to ask strangers ten cents apiece, and I scratched along somehow till this man came round and heard of me, and he offered me my keep and good pay to go along with him. He had another giantess before me, but she had begun to fall away consider'ble, so he paid her off and let her go. This other giantess was an awful expense to him, she was such an eater; now I don't have no great of an appetite,"—this was said plaintively,—"and he 's raised my pay since I 've been with him because we did so well. I took up with his offer because I was nothing but a drag and never will be. I 'm as comfortable as I can be, but it 's a pretty hard business. My oldest boy is able to do for himself, but he 's married this last year, and his wife don't want me. I don't know 's I blame her either. It would be something like if I had a daughter, now; but there, I 'm getting to like traveling first-rate; it gives anybody a good deal to think of."

"I was asking the folks about you when I was up home the early part of the summer," said Mrs. Kew, "but all they knew was that you were living out in New York State. Have you been living in Kentucky long? I saw it on the picture outside."

"No," said the giantess, "that was a picture the man bought cheap from another show that broke up last year. It says six hundred and fifty pounds, but I don't weigh more than four hundred. I have n't been weighed for some time past. Between you and me I don't weigh so much as that, but you must n't mention it, for it would spoil my reputation, and might hender my getting another engagement." And then the poor giantess lost her professional look and tone as she said, "I believe I'd rather die than grow any bigger. I do lose heart sometimes, and wish I was a smart woman and could keep house. I'd be smarter than ever I was when I had the chance; I tell you that! Is Thomas along with you?"

"No. I came with these young ladies, Miss Lancaster and Miss Denis, who are stopping over to Deephaven for the summer." Kate and I turned as we heard this introduction; we were standing close by, and I am proud to say that I never saw Kate treat any one more politely than she did that absurd, pitiful creature with the gilt crown and many bracelets. It was not that she said much, but there was such an exquisite courtesy in her manner, and an apparent unconsciousness of there being anything in the least surprising or uncommon about the giantess.

Just then a party of people came in, and Mrs. Kew said good-by reluctantly. "It has done me sights of good to see you," said our new acquaintance. "I was feeling downhearted just before you came in. I'm pleased to see somebody that remembers me as I used to be." And they shook hands in a way that meant a great deal; and when

Kate and I said good afternoon, the giantess looked at us gratefully, and said, "I 'm very much obliged to you for coming in, young ladies."

"Walk in! walk in!" the man was shouting as we came away. "Walk in and see the wonder of the world, ladies and gentlemen, — the largest woman ever seen in America, — the great Kentucky giantess!"

"Would n't you have liked to stay longer?" Kate asked Mrs. Kew as we came down the street. But she answered that it would be no satisfaction; the people were coming in, and she would have no chance to talk. "I never knew her very well; she is younger than I, and used to go to meeting where I did, but she lived five or six miles from our house. She 's had a hard time of it, according to her account," said Mrs. Kew. "She used to be a dreadful flighty, high-tempered girl, but she 's lost that now, I can see by her eye. I was running it over in my mind to see if there was anything I could do for her, but I don't know as there is. She said the man who hired her was kind. I guess your treating her so polite did her as much good as anything. She used to be real ambitious. I had it on my tongue's end to ask her if she could n't get a few days' leave and come out to stop with me, but I thought just in time that she 'd sink the dory in a minute if she shifted quick. There! seeing her has took away all the fun," said Mrs. Kew ruefully; and we were all dismal for a while, but at last, after we were fairly started for home, we began to be merry again.

We passed the Craper family, whom we had seen at the store in the morning; the children looked as stupid as ever, but the father, I am sorry to say, had been tempted to drink more bad whiskey than was good for him. He had a bright flush on his cheeks, and was flourishing his whip, and hoarsely singing some meaningless tune. "Poor creature!" said I, "I should think this day's pleasuring would kill him."

"Now, should n't you think so?" said Mrs. Kew sympathizingly. "But the truth is, you could n't kill one of them Crapers if you pounded him in a mortar."

We had a pleasant drive home, and kept Mrs. Kew to supper, and afterward went down to the shore to see her set sail for home. Mr. Kew had come in some time before, and had been waiting for the moon to rise. Mrs. Kew told us that she should have enough to think of for a year, she had enjoyed the day so much; and we stood on the pebbles, watching the boat out of the harbor, and wishing ourselves on board, it was such a beautiful evening.

We went to another show that summer, the memory of which will never fade. It is somewhat impertinent to call it a show, and "public entertainment" is equally inappropriate, though we certainly were entertained. It had been raining for two or three days; the Deephaveners spoke of it as "a spell of weather." Just after tea one Thursday evening, Kate and I went down to the post-office. When we opened the great hall door, the salt air was delicious, but we found the town apparently wet through and discouraged; and though it had almost stopped raining just then, there was a Scotch mist, like a snow-storm with the chill taken off, and the Chantrey elms dripped hurriedly, and creaked occasionally in the east wind.

"There will not be a cap'n on the wharves for a week after this," said I to Kate; "only think of the cases of rheumatism!"

We stopped for a few minutes at the Carews', who were as much surprised to see us as if we had been mermaids out of the sea, and begged us to give ourselves something warm to drink, and to change our boots the moment we got home. Then we went on to the post-office. Kate went in, but stopped, as she came out with our letters, to

The Lecture Notice

read a written notice securely fastened to the grocery door by four large carpet-tacks with wide leathers round their necks.

"Dear," said she exultantly, "there 's going to be a lecture to-night in the church, — a free lecture on the 'Elements of True Manhood.' Would n't you like to go?" And we went.

We were fifteen minutes later than the time appointed, and were sorry to find that the audience was almost imperceptible. The dampness had affected the antiquated lamps so that those on the walls and on the front of the gallery were the dimmest lights I ever saw, and sent their feeble rays through a small space the edges of which were clearly defined. There were two rather more energetic lights on the table near the pulpit, where the lecturer sat; and as we were in the rear of the church, we could see the yellow fog between ourselves and him. There were fourteen persons in the audience, and we were all huddled together in a cowardly way in the pews nearest the door: three old men, four women, and four children, besides ourselves and the sexton, a deaf little old man with a wooden leg.

The children whispered noisily, and soon, to our surprise, the lecturer rose and began. He bowed, and treated us with beautiful deference, and read his dreary lecture with enthusiasm. I wish I could say, for his sake, that it was interesting; but I cannot tell a lie, and it was so long! He went on and on, until it seemed as if I had been there ever since I was a little girl. Kate and I did not dare to look at each other, and in my desperation at feeling her quiver with laughter, I moved to the other end of the pew, knocking over a big hymn-book on the way, which attracted so much attention that I have seldom felt more embarrassed in my life. Kate's great dog rose several times to shake himself and yawn loudly, and then lie down again despairingly.

You would have thought the man was addressing an enthusiastic Young Men's Christian Association. He exhorted with fervor upon our duties as citizens and as voters, and told us a great deal about George Washington and Benjamin Franklin, whom he urged us to choose as our examples. He waited for applause after each of his outbursts of eloquence, and presently went on again, in no wise disconcerted at the silence, and as if he were sure that he would fetch us next time. The rain began to fall again heavily, and the wind wailed around the meeting-house. If the lecture had been upon any other subject, it would not have been so hard for Kate and me to keep sober faces; but it was directed entirely toward young men, and there was not a young man there.

The children in front of us mildly scuffled with each other at one time, until the one at the end of the pew dropped a marble, which struck the floor and rolled with a frightful noise down the edge of the aisle where there was no carpet. The congregation instinctively started up to look after it, but we recollected ourselves and leaned back again in our places, while the awed children, after keeping unnaturally quiet, fell asleep, and tumbled against each other helplessly. After a time the man sat down and wiped his forehead, looking well satisfied; and when we were wondering whether we might with propriety come away, he rose again, and said it was a free lecture, and he thanked us for our kind patronage on that inclement night; but in other places which he had visited there had been a contribution taken up for the cause. It would, perhaps, do no harm, — would the sexton —

But the sexton could not have heard the sound of a cannon at that distance, and slumbered on. Neither Kate nor I had any money, except a twenty-dollar bill in my purse, and some coppers in the pocket of her water-proof cloak which she assured me she was prepared to give; but we saw no signs of the sexton's waking, and as one of the women kindly went forward to wake the children, we all rose and came away.

After we had made as much fun and laughed as long as we pleased that night, we became suddenly conscious of the pitiful side of it all; and being anxious that every one should have the highest opinion of Deephaven, we sent Tom Dockum early in the morning with an anonymous note to the lecturer, whom he found without much trouble; but afterward we were disturbed at hearing that he was going to repeat his lecture that evening, — the wind having gone round to the northwest, — and I have no doubt there were a good many women able to be out, and that he harvested enough ten-cent pieces to pay his expenses without our help; though he had particularly told us it was for "the cause," the evening before, and that ought to have been a consolation.

Cunner-Fishing

ONE of the chief pleasures in Deephaven was our housekeeping. Going to market was apt to use up a whole morning, especially if we went to the fish-houses. We depended somewhat upon supplies from Boston, but sometimes we used to chase a butcher who took a drive in his old canvas-topped cart when he felt like it ; and as for fish, there were always enough to be caught, even if we could not buy any. Our acquaintances would often ask if we had anything for dinner that day, and would kindly suggest that somebody had been boiling lobsters, or that a boat had just come in with some nice mackerel, or that somebody over on the Ridge was calculating to kill a lamb, and we had better speak for a quarter in good season. I am afraid we were looked upon as being in danger of becoming epicures, which we certainly are not, and we undoubtedly roused a great deal of interest because we used to eat mushrooms, which grew in the suburbs of the town in wild luxuriance.

One morning Maggie told us that there was nothing in the house for dinner, and, taking an early start, we went at once down to the store to ask if the butcher had been seen, but finding that he had gone out deep-sea fishing for two days, and that when he came back he had planned to kill a veal, we left word for a sufficient piece of the doomed animal to be set apart for our family, and strolled down to the shore to see if we could find some mackerel; but there was not a fisherman in sight, and after going to all the fish-houses we concluded that we had better provide for ourselves. We had not brought our own lines, but we knew where Danny kept his; and after finding a basket of suitable size, and taking some clams from Danny's bait-tub, we went over to the hull of an old schooner which was going to pieces alongside one of the ruined wharves. We looked down the hatchway into the hold, and could see the flounders and sculpin swimming about lazily, and once in a while a little pollock scooted down among them impertinently and then disappeared. "There is that same big flounder that we saw day before yesterday," said I. "I know him, because one of his fins is half gone. I don't believe he can get out, for the hole in the side of the schooner is n't very wide, and is higher up than flounders ever swim. Perhaps he came in when he was young, and was too lazy to go out until he was so large he could n't. Flounders always look so lazy, and as if they thought a great deal of themselves."

"I hope they will think enough of themselves to keep away from my hook this morning," said Kate philosophically, "and the sculpin too. I am going to fish for cunners alone, and keep my line short." And she perched herself on the quarter, baited her hook carefully, and threw it over, with a clam-shell to call attention. I went to the rail at the side, and we were presently much encouraged by pulling up two small cunners, and felt that our prospects for dinner were excellent. Then I unhappily caught so large a sculpin that it was like pulling up an open umbrella; and after I had thrown him into the hold to keep company with the flounder, our usual good luck seemed to desert us. It was one of the days when, in spite of twitching the line and using all the tricks we could think of, the cunners would either eat our bait or keep away altogether. Kate at last said we must starve unless we could catch the big flounder, and asked me to drop my hook down the hatchway; but it seemed almost too bad to destroy his innocent happiness. Just then we heard the noise of oars, and to our delight saw Cap'n Sands in his dory just beyond the next wharf. "Any luck?" said he. "S'pose ye don't care anything about going out this morning?"

"We are not amusing ourselves; we are trying to catch some fish for dinner," said Kate. "Could you wait out by the red buoy while we get a few more, and then should you be back by noon, or are you going for a longer voyage, Captain Sands?"

"I was going out to Black Rock for cunners myself," said the cap'n. "I should be pleased to take ye, if ye'd like to go." So we wound up our lines, and took our basket and clams, and went round to meet the boat. I felt like rowing, and took the oars while Kate was mending her sinker and the cap'n was busy with a snarled line.

"It 's pretty hot," said he presently, "but I see a breeze coming in, and the clouds seem to be thickening; I guess we shall have it cooler 'long towards noon. It looked last night as if we were going to have foul weather, but the scud seemed to blow off, and it was as pretty a morning as ever I see. 'A growing moon chaws up the clouds,' my gran'ther used to say. He was as knowing about the weather as anybody I ever come across; 'most always hit it just about right. Some folks lay all the weather to the moon, accordin' to where she quarters, and when she's in perigee we're going to have this kind of weather, and when she's in apogee she's got to do so and so for sartain; but gran'ther, he used to laugh at all them things. He said it never made no kind of difference, and he went by the looks of the clouds and the feel of the air, and he thought folks could n't make no kind of rules that held good, that had to do with the moon. Well, he did use to depend on the moon some; everybody knows we are n't so likely to have foul weather in a growing moon as we be when she's waning. But some folks I could name, they can't do nothing without having the moon's opinion on it. When I went my second voyage afore the mast, we was in port ten days at Cadiz, and the ship, she needed salting dreadful. The mate kept telling the captain how low the salt was in her, and we was going a long voyage from there; but no, he would n't have her salted nohow, because it was the wane of the moon. He was an amazing set kind of man, the cap'n was, and would have his own way on sea or shore. The mate was his own brother, and they used to fight like a cat and dog; they owned most of the ship between 'em. I was slushing the mizzen-mast, and heard 'em a-disputin' about the salt. The cap'n was a first-rate seaman and died rich, but he was dreadful notional. I know one time we were a-lyin' out in the stream all ready to weigh anchor, and everything was in trim, the men were up in the rigging, and a fresh breeze going out, just what we'd been waiting for, and the word was passed to take in sail and make everything fast. The men swore, and everybody said the cap'n had had some kind of a warning. But that night it began to blow, and I tell you afore morning we were glad enough we were in harbor. The old Victor, she dragged her anchor, and the fore-to'-gallant sail and r'yal got loose somehow and was blown out of the bolt-ropes. Most of the canvas and rigging was old, but we had first-rate weather after that, and did n't bend near all the new sail we had aboard, though the cap'n was 'most afraid we'd come short when we left Boston. That was 'most sixty year ago," said the captain reflectively. "How time does slip away! You young folks have n't any idea. She was a first-rate ship, the old Victor was, though I suppose she would n't cut much of a dash now 'longside of some of the new clippers.

"There used to be some strange-looking

The Hannah

crafts in those days; there was the old brig Hannah. They used to say she would sail backwards as fast as forwards; and she was so square in the bows, they used to call her the sugar-box. She was master old, the Hannah was, and there was n't a port from here to New Orleans where she was n't known; she used to carry a master cargo for her size, more than some ships that ranked two hundred and fifty ton, and she was put down for two hundred. She used to make good voyages, the Hannah did; and then there was the Pactolus, she was just about such another, — you would have laughed to see her. She sailed out of this port for a good many years. Cap'n Wall, he told me that if he had her before the wind with a cargo of cotton, she would make a middling good run; but load her deep with salt, and you might as well try to sail a stick of oak timber with a handkerchief. She was a stout-built ship: I should n't wonder if her timbers were afloat somewhere yet; she was sold to some parties out in San Francisco. There! everything 's changed from what it was when I used to follow the sea. I wonder sometimes if the sailors have as queer works aboard ship as they used. Bless ye! Deephaven used to be a different place to what it is now; there was hardly a day in the year that you did n't hear the shipwrights' hammers, and there was always something going on at the wharves. You would see the folks from up country comin' in with their loads of oak knees and plank, and logs o' rock-maple for keels when there was snow on the ground in winter-time, and the big sticks of timber-pine for masts would come crawling along the road with their three and four yoke of oxen all frosted up, the sleds creaking and the snow growling and the men flapping their arms to keep warm, and hallooing as if there wa'n't nothin' else goin' on in the world except to get them masts to the ship-yard. Bless ye! two o' them teams together would stretch from here 'most up to the Widow Jim's place, — no such timber-pines nowadays."

"I suppose the sailors are very jolly together sometimes," said Kate meditatively, with the least flicker of a smile at me. The captain did not answer for a minute, as he was battling with an obstinate snarl in his line; but when he had found the right loop, he said: "I 've had the best times and the hardest times of my life at sea, that 's certain! I was just thinking it over when you spoke. I 'll tell you some tales one day or 'nother that 'll please you. Land! you 've no idea what tricks some of those wild fellows will be up to. Now, saying they fetch home a cargo of wines and they want a drink; they 've got a trick so they can get it. Saying it 's champagne, they 'll fetch up a basket, and how do you suppose they 'll get into it?"

Of course we did n't know.

"Well, every basket will be counted, and they 're fastened up particular, so they can tell in a minute if they 've been tampered with; and neither must you draw the corks if you could get the basket open. I suppose ye may have seen champagne, how it 's all wired and waxed. Now, they take a clean tub, them fellows do, and just shake the basket and jounce it up and down till they break the bottles and let the wine drain out; then they take it down in the hold and put it back with the rest, and when the cargo is delivered there 's only one or two whole bottles in that basket, and there 's a dreadful fuss about its being stowed so foolish." The captain told this with an air of great satisfaction, but we did not show the least suspicion that he might have assisted at some such festivity.

"Then they have a smart way of breaking into a cask. It won't do to start the bung, and it won't do to bore a hole where it can be seen, but they 're up to that: they slip back one of the end hoops and bore two holes underneath it, — one for the air to go in and one for the liquor to come out, — and after they get all out they want, they put in some spigots and cut them down close to the stave, knock back the hoop again, and there ye are, all trig."

"I never should have thought of it," said Kate admiringly.

"There is n't nothing," Cap'n Sands went on, "that 'll hender some masters from cheating the owners a little. Get them off in a foreign port, and there 's nobody to watch, and the most of them have a feeling that they ain't getting full pay, and they 'll charge things to the ship that she never seen nor heard of. There were two shipmasters that sailed out of Salem. I heard one of 'em tell the story. They had both come into port from Liverpool nigh the same time, and one of 'em, he was dressed up in a handsome suit of clothes, and the other looked kind of poverty-struck. 'Where did you get them clothes?' says he. 'Why, to Liverpool,' says the other; 'you don't meant to say you come away without none, cheap as cloth was there?' 'Why, yes,' says the other cap'n; 'I can't afford to wear such clothes as those be, and I don't see how you can, either.' 'Charge 'em to the ship, bless ye; the owners expect it.'

"So the next v'y'ge the poor cap'n, he had a nice double rig for himself made to the best tailor's in Bristol, and charged it, say ten pounds, in the ship's account; and when he came home, the ship's husband, he was looking over the papers, and 'What 's this?' says he, 'how come the ship to run up a tailor's bill?' 'Why, them 's mine,' says the cap'n, very meaching. 'I onderstood that there would n't be no objection made.' 'Well, you made a mistake,' says the other, laughing; 'guess I 'd better scratch this out.' And it was n't long before the cap'n met the one who had put him up to doing it, and he give him a blowing up for getting him into such a fix. 'Land sakes alive!' says he, 'were you fool enough to set it down in the account? Why, I put mine in for so many bolts of Russia duck.'"

Captain Sands seemed to enjoy this reminiscence, and to our satisfaction, in a few minutes, after he had offered to take the oars, he went on to tell us another story.

"Why, as for cheating, there 's plenty of that all over the world. The first v'y'ge I went into Havana as master of the Deerhound, she had never been in the port before, and had to be measured and recorded, and then pay her tonnage duties every time she went into port there afterward, according to what she was registered on the customhouse books. The inspector, he come aboard, and he went below and looked all round, and he measured her between decks; but he never offered to set down any figgers, and

The Lighthouse

when we came back into the cabin, says he, 'Yes — yes — good ship! you put one doubloon front of this eye, *so!*' says he, 'an' I not see with him; and you put one more doubloon front of other eye, and how you think I see at all what figger you write?' So I took his book and I set down her measurements, and made her out twenty ton short, and he took his doubloons and shoved 'm into his pocket. There, it is n't what you call straight dealing, but everybody done it that dared, and you 'd eat up all the profits of a v'y'ge, and the owners would just as soon you 'd try a little up-country air, if you paid all those dues according to law. Tonnage was dreadful high, and wharfage, too, in some ports, and they 'd get your last cent some way or 'nother if ye were n't sharp.

"Old Cap'n Carew, uncle to them ye see to meeting, did a smart thing in the time of the embargo. Folks got tired of it, and it was dreadful hard times — ships rotting at the wharves; and Deephaven never was quite the same afterward, though the old place held out for a good while before she let go as ye see her now. You 'd 'a' had a hard grip on 't when I was a young man to make me believe it would ever be so dull here. Well, Cap'n Carew, he bought an old brig that was lying over by East Parish, and he began fitting her up and loading her for the West Indies; and the farmers they 'd come in there by night from all round the country, to sell salt-fish and lumber and potatoes, and glad enough they were, I tell ye. The rigging was put in order, and it was n't long before she was ready to sail, and it was all kept mighty quiet. She lay up to an old wharf in a cove where she would n't be much noticed, and they took care not to paint her any or to attract any attention.

"One day Cap'n Carew was over in Riverport dining out with some gentlemen, and the revenue officer sat next to him, and by and by says he, 'Why won't ye take a ride with me this afternoon? I 've had warning that there 's a brig loading for the West Indies over beyond Deephaven somewheres, and I 'm going over to seize her.' And he laughed to himself as if he expected fun, and something in his pocket beside. Well, the first minute that Cap'n Carew dared, after dinner, he slipped out, and he hired the swiftest horse in Riverport and rode for dear life, and told the folks who were in the secret and some who were n't what was the matter, and every soul turned to and helped finish loading her and getting the rigging ready and the water aboard; but just as they were leaving the cove — the wind was blowing just right — along came the revenue officer with two or three men, and they came off in a boat and boarded her as important as could be.

"'Won't ye step into the cabin, gentlemen, and take a glass o' wine?' says Cap'n Carew, very polite; and the wind came in fresher, — something like a squall for a few minutes, — and the men had the sails spread before you could say Jack Robi'son; and before those fellows knew what they were about, the old brig was a-standing out to sea, and the folks on the wharves cheered and yelled. The cap'n gave the officers a good scare and offered 'em a free passage to the West Indies, and finally they said they would n't report at headquarters if he 'd let 'em go ashore. So he told the sailors to lower their boat about two miles off Deephaven, and they pulled ashore meek enough. Cap'n Carew had a first-rate run, and made a lot of money, so I have heard it said. Bless ye! every shipmaster would have done just the same if he had dared, and everybody was glad when they heard about it. Dreadful foolish piece of business that embargo was!

"Now I declare," said Captain Sands, after he had finished this narrative, "here I 'm a-telling stories and you 're doin' all the work. You 'll pull a boat ahead of anybody if you keep on. Tom Kew was a-praisin' up both of you to me the other day; says he, 'They don't put on no airs, but I tell ye they can pull a boat well, and swim like fish,' says he. There, now, if you 'll give me the oars, I 'll put the dory just where I want her, and you can be getting your lines ready. I know a place here where it 's always toler'ble fishing, and I guess we 'll get something."

Kate and I cracked our clams on the gunwale of the boat, and cut them into nice little bits for bait with a piece of the shell; and by the time the captain had thrown out the killick we were ready to begin, and found the fishing much more exciting than it had been at the wharf.

"I don't know as I ever see 'em bite faster," said the old sailor presently; "guess it 's because they like the folks that 's fishing. Well, I 'm pleased. I thought I 'd let 'Bijah take some along to Denby in the cart to-morrow, if I got more than I could use at home. I did n't calc'late on having such a lively crew aboard. I s'pose ye would n't care about going out a little further by and by, to see if we can't get two or three haddock?" And we answered that we should like nothing better.

It was growing cloudy, and was much cooler, — the perfection of a day for fishing, — and we sat there diligently pulling in cunners, and talking a little once in a while. The tide was nearly out, and Black Rock looked almost large enough to be called an island. The sea was smooth, and the low waves broke lazily among the seaweed-covered ledges, while our boat swayed about on the water, lifting and falling gently as the waves went in shore. We were not a very long way from the lighthouse, and once we could see Mrs. Kew's big white apron as she stood in the doorway for a few minutes. There was no noise except the plash of the low-tide waves and the occasional flutter of a fish in the bottom of the dory. Kate and I always killed our fish at once by a rap on the head, for it certainly saved the poor creatures much discomfort, and ourselves as well, and it made it easier to take them off the hook than if they were flopping about and making us aware of our cruelty.

Suddenly the captain wound up his line and said he thought we 'd better be going in, and Kate and I looked at him with surprise. "It is only half-past ten," said I, looking at my watch. "Don't hurry in on our account," added Kate persuasively, for we were having a very good time.

"I guess we won't mind about the haddock. I 've got a feelin' we 'd better go ashore." And he looked up into the sky and turned to see the west. "I knew there was something the matter; there 's going to be a shower." And we looked behind us to see a bank of heavy clouds coming over fast. "I wish we had two pair of oars," said Captain Sands. I 'm afraid we shall get caught."

Landing the Dory

"You need n't mind us," said Kate. "We are n't in the least afraid of our clothes, and we don't get cold when we 're wet; we have made sure of that." "Well, I 'm glad to hear that," said the cap'n. "Women-folks are apt to be dreadful scared of a wetting; but I 'd just as lief not get wet myself. I had a twinge of rheumatism yesterday. I guess we 'll get ashore fast enough. No, I feel well enough to-day, but you can row if you want to, and I 'll take the oars the last part of the way."

When we reached the moorings, the clouds were black, and the thunder rattled and boomed over the sea, while heavy spatters of rain were already falling. We did not go to the wharves, but stopped down the shore at the fish-houses, the nearer place of shelter. "You just select some of those cunners," said the captain, who was beginning to be a little out of breath, "and then you can run right up and get under cover, and I 'll put a bit of old sail over the rest of the fish to keep the fresh water off." By the time the boat touched the shore and we had pulled it up on the pebbles, the rain had begun in good earnest. Luckily there was a barrow lying near, and we loaded that in a hurry, and just then the captain caught sight of a well-known red shirt in an open door, and shouted, "Halloa, Danny! lend us a hand with these fish, for we 're nigh on to being shipwrecked." And then we ran up to the fish-house and waited awhile, though we stood in the doorway watching the lightning, and there were so many leaks in the roof that we might almost as well have been out of doors. It was one of Danny's quietest days, and he silently beheaded hake, only winking at us once very gravely at something our other companion said.

"There!" said Captain Sands, "folks may say what they have a mind to; I did n't see that shower coming up, and I know as well as I want to that my wife did, and impressed it on my mind. Our house sets high, and she watches the sky, and is al'ays a-worrying when I go out fishing, for fear something 's going to happen to me, 'specially sence I 've got to be along in years."

This was just what Kate and I wished to hear, for we had been told that Captain Sands had most decided opinions on dreams and other mysteries, and could tell some stories which were considered incredible by even a Deephaven audience, to whom the marvelous was of every-day occurrence.

"Then it has happened before?" asked

Kate. "I wondered why you started so suddenly to come in."

"Happened!" said the captain. "Bless ye, yes! I 'll tell you my views about these p'ints one o' those days. I 've thought a good deal about 'em by spells. Not that I can explain 'em, nor anybody else; but it 's no use to laugh at 'em, as some folks do. Cap'n Lant — you know Cap'n Lant? — he and I have talked it over consider'ble, and he says to me, 'Everybody 's got some story of the kind they will believe in spite of everything, and yet they won't believe yourn.'"

Skipper Scudder

The shower seemed to be over now, and we felt compelled to go home, as the captain did not go on with his remarks. I hope he did not see Danny's wink. Skipper Scudder, who was Danny's friend and partner, came up just then and asked us if we knew what the sign was when the sun came out through the rain.

I said that I had always heard it would rain again next day. "Oh no," said Skipper Scudder, "the Devil is beating his wife."

After dinner, Kate and I went for a walk through some pine woods, which were beautiful after the rain; the mosses and lichens which had been dried up were all freshened and blooming out in the dampness. The smell of the wet pitch-pines was unusually sweet; and we wandered about for an hour or two there, to find some ferns we wanted, and then walked over toward East Parish, and home by the long beach late in the afternoon. We came as far as the boat-landing, meaning to go home through the lane; but to our delight we saw Captain Sands sitting alone on an old overturned whale-boat, whittling busily at a piece of dried kelp. "Good evenin'," said our friend cheerfully. And we explained that we had taken a long walk and thought we would rest awhile before we went home to supper. Kate perched herself on the boat, and I sat down on a ship's knee which lay on the pebbles.

"Did n't get any hurt from being out in the shower, I hope?"

"No, indeed," laughed Kate, "and we had such a good time. I hope you won't mind taking us out again some time."

"Bless ye! no," said the captain. "My girl Lo'isa, she that 's Mis' Winslow over to Riverport, used to go out with me a good deal, and it seemed natural to have you aboard. I missed Lo'isa after she got married, for she was al'ays ready to go anywhere 'long of father. She 's had slim health of late years. I tell 'em she 's been too much shut up out of the fresh air and sun. When she was young her mother never could pr'vail on her to set in the house stiddy and sew, and she used to have great misgivin's that Lo'isa never was going to be capable. How about those fish you caught this morning? good, were they? Mis' Sands had dinner on the stocks when I got home, and she said she would n't fry any 'til supper-time; but I calc'lated to have 'em this noon. I like 'em best right out o' the water. Little more and we should have got them wet. That 's one of my whims; I can't bear to let fish get rained on."

"O Captain Sands!" said I, there being a convenient pause, "you were speaking of your wife just now; did you ask her if she saw the shower?"

"First thing she spoke of when I got into the house. 'There,' says she, 'I was afraid you would n't see the rain coming in time, and I had my heart in my mouth when it began to thunder. I thought you 'd get soaked through, and be laid up for a fortnight,' says she. 'I guess a summer shower won't hurt an old sailor like me,' says I." And the captain reached for another piece of his kelp-stalk, and whittled away more busily than ever. Kate took out her knife and also began to cut kelp, and I threw pebbles in the hope of hitting a spider which sat complacently on a stone not far away; and when he suddenly vanished, there was nothing for me to do but to whittle kelp also.

"Do you suppose," said Kate, "that Mrs. Sands really made you know about that shower?"

The captain put on his most serious look, coughed slowly, and moved himself a few inches nearer us, along the boat. I think he fully understood the importance and solemnity of the occasion. "It ain't for us to say what we do know or don't, for there 's nothing sartain; but I made up my mind long ago that there 's something about these p'ints that 's myster'ous. My wife and me will be sitting there to home, and there won't be no word between us for an hour, and then of a sudden we'll speak up about the same thing. Now the way I view it, she either puts it into my head or I into hers. I 've spoke up lots of times about something, when I did n't know what I was going to say when I began, and she 'll say she was just thinking of that. Like as not you have noticed it sometimes? There was something my mind was dwellin' on yesterday, and she come right out with it, and I 'd a good deal rather she had n't," said the captain ruefully. "I did n't want to rake it all over ag'in, *I* 'm sure." And then he recollected himself, and was silent, which his audience must confess to have regretted for a moment.

"I used to think a good deal about such things when I was younger, and I 'm free to say I took more stock in dreams and such like than I do now. I rec'lect old Parson Lorimer — this Parson Lorimer's father who was settled here first — spoke to me once about it, and said it was a tempting of Providence, and that we had n't no right to pry into secrets. I know I had a dream-book then, that I picked up in a shop in Bristol once when I was in there on the Ranger, and all the young folks were beset to get sight of it. I see what fools it made of folks, bothering their heads about such things, and I pretty much let them go; all this stuff about spirit-rappings is enough to make a man crazy. You don't get no good by it. I come across a paper once with a lot of letters in it from sperits, and I cast my eye over 'em, and I say to myself, 'Well, I always was given to understand that when we come to a futur' state we was goin' to have more wisdom than we can get afore;' but them letters had n't any more sense to 'em, nor so much, as a man could write here without schooling; and I should think that if the folks who wrote 'em had any kind of ambition, they 'd want to be movin' back here again. But as for one person's having something to do with another any distance off, why, that 's another thing; there ain't any nonsense about that. I know it 's true jest as well as I want to," said the cap'n, warming up. "I 'll tell ye how I was led to make up my mind about it. One time I waked a man up out of a sound sleep looking at him, and it set me to thinking. First, there was n't any noise, and then, ag'in, there was n't any touch so he could feel it, and I says to myself, 'Why could n't I ha' done it the width of two rooms as well as one, and why could n't I ha' done it with my back turned?' It could n't have been the looking so much as the thinking. And then I car'd it further, and I says, 'Why ain't a mile as good as a yard? and it 's the thinking that does it,' says I, 'and we 've got some faculty or other that we don't know much about. We 've got some way of sending our thought like a bullet goes out of a gun, and it hits and we can kind of hear what other folks is thinking of. We don't know nothing except what we see. And some folks is scared, and more thinks it is all nonsense and laughs. But there 's something we have n't got the hang of.' It makes me think o' them little black polliwogs that turns into frogs in the fresh-water puddles in the ma'sh. There 's a time before their tails drop off and their legs have sprouted out, but they don't get any use o' their legs, and I dare say they 're in their way consider'ble; but after they get to be frogs they find out what they 're for without no kind of trouble. I guess we shall turn these fac'lties to account some time or 'nother. Seems to me, though, that we might depend on 'em now more than we do."

The captain was under full sail on what we had heard was his pet subject, and it was a great satisfaction to listen to what he had to say. It loses a great deal in being written, for the old sailor's voice and gestures and thorough earnestness all carried no little persuasion. And it was impossible not to be sure that he knew more than people usually do about these mysteries in which he delighted.

"Now, how can you account for this?" said he. "I remember not more than ten years ago my son's wife was stopping at our house, and she had left her child at home while she come away for a rest. And after she had been there two or three days, one morning she was sitting in the kitchen 'long o' the folks, and all of a sudden she jumped out of her chair and ran into the bedroom, and next minute she come out laughing, and looking kind of scared. 'I could ha' taken my oath,' says she, 'that I heard Katy cryin' out *mother!*' says she, 'just as if she was hurt. I heard it so plain that before I stopped to think it seemed as if she were right in the next room. I 'm afeard something has happened.' But the folks laughed, and said she must ha' heard one of the lambs. 'No, it was n't,' says she; 'it was my Katy.' And sure enough, just after dinner a young man who lived neighbor to her come riding into the yard post-haste to get her to go home; for the baby had pulled some hot water over on to herself, and was nigh scalded to death, and cryin' for her mother every minute. Now, who 's going to explain that? It was n't any common hearing that heard that child's cryin'

Captain Sands telling Stories

fifteen miles. And I can tell you another thing that happened among my own folks. There was an own cousin of mine married to a man by the name of John Hathorn. He was trading up to Parsonsfield, and business run down, so he wound up there, and thought he 'd make a new start. He moved down to Denby; and while he was getting under way, he left his family up to the old place, and at the time I speak of was going to move 'em down in about a fortnight.

"One morning his wife was fidgeting round, and finally she came downstairs with her bonnet and shawl on, and said somebody must put the horse right into the wagon and take her down to Denby. 'Why, what for, mother?' they says. 'Don't stop to talk,' says she; 'your father is sick, and wants me. It 's been a-worrying me since before day, and I can't stand it no longer.' And the short of the story is that she kept hurrying 'em faster and faster, and then she got hold of the reins herself, and when they got within five miles of the place the horse fell dead, and she was nigh about crazy, and they took another horse at a farm-house on the road. It was the spring of the year, and the going was dreadful, and when they got to the house John Hathorn had just died, and he had been calling for his wife up to 'most the last breath he drew. He had been taken sick sudden the day before; but the folks knew it was bad traveling, and that she was a feeble woman to come near thirty miles, and they had no idee he was so bad off. I 'm telling you the living truth," said Captain Sands, with an emphatic shake of his head. "There 's more folks than me can tell about it; and if you were goin' to keel-haul me next minute, and hang me to the yard-arm afterward, I could n't say it different. I was up to Parsonsfield to the funeral; it was just after I quit following the sea. I never saw a woman so broke down as she was. John was a nice man, stiddy and pleasant-spoken, and straightforrard and kind to his folks. He belonged to the Odd Fellows, and they all marched to the funeral. There was a good deal of respect shown him, I tell ye.

"There is another story I 'd like to have ye hear, if it 's so that you ain't beat out hearing me talk. When I get going, I slip along as easy as a schooner wing-and-wing afore the wind.

"This happened to my own father, but I never heard him say much about it; never could get him to talk it over to any length, best I could do. But gran'ther, his father, told me about it nigh upon fifty times, first and last, and always the same way. Gran'ther lived to be old, and there was ten or a dozen years after his wife died that he lived year and year about with Uncle Tobias's folks and our folks. Uncle Tobias lived over on the Ridge. I got home from my first v'y'ge as mate of the Daylight just in time for his funeral. I was disapp'inted to find the old man was gone. I 'd fetched him some first-rate tobacco, for he was a great hand to smoke, and I was calc'latin' on his being pleased: old folks like to be thought of, and then he set more by me than by the other boys. I know I used to be sorry for him when I was a little fellow. My father's second wife, she was a well-meaning woman, but an awful driver with her work, and she was always making of him feel he was n't no use. I do' know as she meant to, either. He never said nothing, and he was always just so pleasant, and he was fond of his book, and used to set round reading, and tried to keep himself out of the way just as much as he could. There was one winter when I was small that I had the scarlet-fever, and was very slim for a long time afterward, and I used to keep along o' gran'ther, and he would tell me his old stories. Father 'd been a sailor, — it runs in our blood to foller the sea, — and he 'd been wrecked two or three times and been taken by the Algerine pirates, but he 'd never tell us things like gran'ther. You remind me to tell you some time about the pirates. I wonder if you ever heard about old Citizen Leigh, that used to be about here when I was a boy. He was taken by the Algerines once, same 's father, and they was dreadful f'erce just then, and they sent him home to get the ransom money for the crew; but it was a monstrous price they asked, and the owners would n't give it to him, for they s'posed likely the men was dead by that time, any way. Old Citizen Leigh, he went crazy, and used to go about the streets with a bundle of papers in his hands year in and year out. I 've seen him a good many times. Gran'ther used to tell me how he escaped. I 'll remember it for ye some day if you 'll put me in mind.

"I got to be mate when I was twenty, and I was as strong a fellow as you could scare up, and darin'! — why, it makes my blood run cold when I think of the reckless things I used to do. I was off to sea after I was fifteen year old, and there was n't anybody so glad to see me as gran'ther when I came home. I expect he used to be lonesome after I went off, but then his mind failed him quite a while before he died. Father was clever to him, and he 'd get him anything he spoke about; but he was n't a man to set round and talk, and he never took notice himself when gran'ther was out of tobacco, so sometimes it would be a day or two. I know better how he used to feel now that I 'm getting to be along in years myself, and likely to be some care to the folks before long. I never could bear to see old folks neglected; nice old men and women who have worked hard in their day and been useful and willin'. I 've seen 'em many a time when they could n't help knowing that the folks would a little rather they 'd be in heaven, and a good respectable headstone put up for 'em in the burying-ground.

"Well, now, I 'm sure I 've forgot what I was going to tell you. Oh, yes; about grandmother dreaming about father when he come home from sea. Well, to go back to the first of it, gran'ther never was rugged; he was to Valley Forge that winter in the Revolutionary War, an' got the rheumatism fastened on to him when he was a young man, and though he lived to be so old, he never could work hard, and never got forehanded; and Aunt Hannah Starbird, over at East Parish, took my sister to fetch up, because she was named for her, and Melinda and Tobias stayed at home with the old folks, and my father went to live with an uncle over in Riverport, whom he was named for. He was in the West India trade and was well off, and he had no children of his own, so they expected he would do well by father. He was dreadful high-tempered. I 've heard say he had the worst temper that was ever raised in Deephaven.

"One day he set father to putting some cherries into a bar'l of rum, and went off down to his wharf to see to the loading of a vessel, and afore he come back father found he'd got hold of the wrong bar'l, and had sp'ilt a bar'l of the best Holland gin; he tried to get the cherries out, but that was n't any use, and he was dreadful afraid of Uncle Matthew, and he run away, and never was heard of from that time out. They supposed he'd run away to sea, as he had a leaning that way, but nobody ever knew for certain; and his mother, she 'most mourned herself to death. Gran'ther told me that it got so at last that if they could only know for sure that he was dead, it was all they would ask. But it went on four years, and gran'ther got used to it some ; though grandmother never would give up. And one morning early, before day, she waked him up, and says she, 'We 're going to hear from Matthew. Get up quick and go down to the store, an' see if there's a letter ! 'Nonsense,' says he. 'I 've seen him,' says grandmother, 'and he 's coming home. He looks older, but just the same other ways, and he 's got long hair, like a horse's mane, all down over his shoulders.' 'Well, let the dead rest,' says gran'ther; 'you 've thought about the boy till your head is turned.' 'I tell you I saw Matthew himself,' says she, 'and I want you to go right down to see if there is n't a letter.' And she kept at him till he saddled the horse, and he got down to the store before it was opened in the morning, and he had to wait round, and when the man came over to unlock it, he was 'most ashamed to tell what his errand was, for he had been so many times, and everybody supposed the boy was dead. When he asked for a letter, the man said there was none there, and asked if he was expecting any particular one. He did n't get many letters, I s'pose ; all his folks lived about here, and people did n't write any to speak of in those days. Gran'ther said he thought he would n't make such a fool of himself again, but he did n't say anything, and he waited round awhile, talking to one and another who came up, and by and by says the storekeeper, who was reading a newspaper that had just come, 'Here 's some news for you, Sands, I do believe! There are three vessels come into Boston harbor that have been out whaling and sealing in the South Seas for three or four years, and your son Matthew's name is down on the list of the crew.' 'I tell ye,' says gran'ther, 'I took that paper, and I got on my horse and put for home, and your grandmother, she hailed me, and she said, "You 've heard, have n't you?" before I told her a word.'

"Gran'ther, he got his breakfast and started right off for Boston, and got there early the second day, and went right down on the wharves. Somebody lent him a boat, and he went out to where there were two sealers laying off riding at anchor, and he asked a sailor if Matthew was aboard. 'Ay, ay,' says the sailor, 'he 's down below.' And he sung out for him; and when he come up out of the hold his hair was long, down over his shoulders, like a horse's mane, just as his mother saw it in the dream. Gran'ther, he did n't know what to say, — it scared him, — and he asked how it happened; and father told how they 'd been off sealing in the South Seas, and he and another man had lived alone on an island for months, and the whole crew had grown wild in their ways of living, being off so long, and for one thing had gone without hats and let their hair grow. The rest of the men had been ashore and got fixed up smart, but he had been busy, and had put it off till that morning; he was just going ashore then. Father was all struck up when he heard about the dream, and said his mind had been dwellin' on his mother and going home, and he come down to let her see him just as he was, and she said it was the same way he looked in the dream. He never would have his hair cut — father would n't — and wore it in a queue. I remember seeing him with it when I was a boy; but his second wife did n't like the looks of it, and she come up behind him one day and cut it off with the scissors. He was terrible worked up about it. I never see father so mad as he was that day. Now this is just as true as the Bible," said Captain Sands. "I have n't put a word to it, and gran'ther al'ays told a story just as it was. That woman saw her son; but if you ask me what kind of eye-sight it was, I can't tell you, nor nobody else."

Later that evening, Kate and I drifted into a long talk about the captain's stories and these mysterious powers of which we know so little. It was somewhat chilly in the house, and we had kindled a fire in the fireplace, which at first made a blaze which lighted the old room royally, and then quieted down into red coals and lazy puffs of smoke. We had carried the lights away, and sat with our feet on the fender, and Kate's great dog was lying between us on the rug. I remember that evening so well; we could see the stars through the window plainer and plainer as the fire went down, and we could hear the noise of the sea.

"Do you remember, in the old myth of Demeter and Persephone," Kate asked me, "where Demeter takes care of the child and gives it ambrosia and hides it in fire, because she loves it and wishes to make it immortal and to give it eternal youth; and then the mother finds it out and cries in terror to hinder her, and the goddess angrily throws the child down and rushes away? And he had to share the common destiny of mankind, though he always had some wonderful inscrutable grace and wisdom, because a goddess had loved him and held him in her arms. I always thought that part of the story beautiful where Demeter throws off her disguise and is no longer an old woman, and the great house is filled with brightness like lightning, and she rushes out through the halls with her yellow hair waving over her shoulders, and the people would give anything to bring her back again, and to undo their mistake. I knew it almost all by heart once," said Kate, "and I am always finding a new meaning in it. I was just thinking that it may be that we all have given to us more or less of another nature, as the child had whom Demeter wished to make like the gods. I believe old Captain Sands is right, and we have these instincts which defy all our wisdom and for which we never can frame any laws. We may laugh at them, but we are always meeting them, and one cannot help knowing that it has been the same through all history. They are powers which are imperfectly developed in this life, but one cannot help the thought that the mystery of this world may be the commonplace of the next."

"I wonder," said I, "why it is that one hears so much more of such things from simple country people. They believe in dreams, and they have a kind of fetichism, and believe so heartily in supernatural causes. I suppose nothing could shake Mrs. Patton's faith in warnings. There is no end of absurdity in it, and yet there is one side of such lives for which one cannot help having reverence ; they live so much nearer to nature than people who are in cities, and there

Bedtime

is often a soberness about country people that one cannot help noticing. I wonder if they are unconsciously awed by the strength and purpose in the world about them, and the mysterious creative power which is at work with them on their familiar farms. In their simple life they take their instincts for truths, and perhaps they are not always so far wrong as we imagine. Because they are so instinctive and unreasoning, they may have a more complete sympathy with Nature, and may hear her voices when wiser ears are deaf. They have much in common, after all, with the plants which grow up out of the ground and the wild creatures which depend upon their instincts wholly."

"I think," said Kate, "that the more one lives out of doors the more personality there seems to be in what we call inanimate things. The strength of the hills and the voice of the waves are no longer only grand poetical sentences, but an expression of something real, and more and more one finds God himself in the world, and believes that we may read the thoughts that He writes for us in the book of Nature." And after this we were silent for a while; and in the mean time it grew very late, and we watched the fire until there were only a few sparks left in the ashes. The stars faded away, and the moon came up out of the sea, and we barred the great hall door and went upstairs to bed. The lighthouse lamp burned steadily, and it was the only light that had not been blown out in all Deephaven.

Mrs. Bonny

I AM sure that Kate Lancaster and I must have spent by far the greater part of the summer out of doors. We often made long expeditions out into the suburbs of Deephaven, sometimes being gone all day, and sometimes taking a long afternoon stroll and coming home early in the evening hungry as hunters and laden with treasure, whether we had been through the pine woods inland or alongshore, whether we had met old friends or made some desirable new acquaintances. We had a fashion of calling at the farm-houses, and by the end of the season we knew as many people as if we had lived in Deephaven all our days. We used to ask for a drink of water; this was our unfailing introduction, and afterward there were many interesting subjects which one could introduce, and we could always give the latest news at the shore. It was amusing to see the curiosity which we aroused. Many of the people came into Deephaven only on special occasions, and I must confess that at first we were often naughty enough to wait until we had been severely cross-questioned before we gave a definite account of ourselves. Kate was very clever at making unsatisfactory answers when she cared to do so. We did not understand, for some time, with what a keen sense of enjoyment many of those people made the acquaintance of an entirely new person who cordially gave the full particulars about herself; but we soon learned to call this by another name than impertinence.

I think there were no points of interest in that region which we did not visit with conscientious faithfulness. There were cliffs and pebble-beaches, the long sands and the short sands; there were Black Rock and Roaring Rock, High Point and East Point, and Spouting Rock; we went to see where a ship had been driven ashore in the night, all hands being lost and not a piece of her left larger than an axe-handle; we visited the spot where a ship had come ashore in the fog, and had been left high and dry on the edge of the marsh when the tide went out; we saw where the brig Methuselah had been wrecked, and the shore had been golden with her cargo of lemons and oranges, which one might carry away by the wherryful.

Inland there were not so many noted localities, but we used to enjoy the woods and our explorations among the farms immensely. To the westward the land was better and the people well-to-do; but we went oftenest toward the hills and among the poorer people. The land was uneven and full of ledges, and the people worked hard for their living, at most laying aside only a few dollars each year. Some of the more enterprising young people went away to work in shops and factories; but the custom was by no means universal, and the people had a hungry, discouraged look. It is all very well to say that they knew nothing better, that it was the only life of which they knew anything; there was too often a look of disappointment in their faces, and sooner or later we heard or guessed many stories: that this young man had wished for an education, but there had been no money to spare for books or schooling ; and that one had meant to learn a trade, but there must be some one to help his father with the farm-work, and there was no money to hire a man to work in his place if he went away. The older people had a hard look, as if they had always to be on the alert and must fight for their place in the world. One could only forgive and pity their petty sharpness, which showed itself in trifling bargains, when one understood how much a single dollar meant where dollars came so rarely. We used to pity the young girls so much. It was plain that those who knew how much easier and pleasanter our lives were could not help envying us.

There was a high hill half a dozen miles from Deephaven which was known in its region as "the mountain." It was the highest land anywhere near us ; and having been told that there was a fine view from the top, one day we went there, with Tommy Dockum for escort. We overtook Mr. Lorimer, the minister, on his way to make parochial calls upon some members of his parish who lived far from church, and to our delight he proposed to go with us instead. It was a great satisfaction to have him for a guide, for he knew both the country and the people more intimately than any one else. It was a long climb to the top of the hill, but not a hard one. The sky was clear, and there was a fresh wind, though we had left none at all at the sea-level. After lunch, Kate and I spread our shawls over a fine cushion of mountain-cranberry, and had a long talk with Mr. Lorimer about ancient and modern Deephaven. He always seemed as much pleased with our enthusiasm for the town as if it had been a personal favor and compliment to himself. I remember how far we could see, that day, and how we looked toward the far-away blue mountains, and then out over the ocean. Deephaven looked insignificant from that height and distance, and indeed the country seemed to be mostly covered with the pointed tops of pines and spruces, and there were long tracts of maple and beech woods with their coloring of lighter, fresher green.

"Suppose we go down, now," said Mr. Lorimer, long before Kate and I had meant to propose such a thing; and our feeling was that of dismay. "I should like to take you to make a call with me. Did you ever hear of old Mrs. Bonny?"

"No," said we, and cheerfully gathered our wraps and baskets; and when Tommy finally came panting up the hill after we had begun to think that our shoutings and whistling were useless, we sent him down to the horses, and went down ourselves by another path. It led us a long distance through a grove of young beeches; the last year's whitish leaves lay thick on the ground, and the new leaves made so close a roof overhead that the light was strangely purple, as if it had come through a great church window of stained glass. After this we went through some hemlock growth, where, on the lower branches, the pale green of the new shoots and the dark green of the old made an exquisite contrast each to the other. Finally we came out at Mrs. Bonny's. Mr. Lorimer had told us something about her on the way down, saying in the first place that she was one of the queerest characters he knew. Her husband used to be a charcoal-burner and basket-maker, and she used to sell butter, and berries, and eggs, and choke-pears preserved in molasses. She always came down to Deephaven on a little black horse, with her goods in baskets and bags which were fastened to the saddle in a mysterious way. She had the reputation of not being a neat housekeeper, and none of the wise women of the town would touch her butter especially, so it was always a joke when she coaxed a new resident or a strange shipmaster into buying her wares; but the old woman always managed to jog home without the freight she had brought. "She must be very old, now," said Mr. Lorimer; "I have not seen her in a long time. It cannot be possible that her horse is still alive!" And we all laughed when we saw Mrs. Bonny's steed at a little distance, for the shaggy old creature was covered with mud, pine-needles, and dead leaves, with half the last year's burdock-burs in all Deephaven snarled into his mane and tail and sprinkled over his fur, which looked nearly as long as a buffalo's. He had hurt his leg, and his kind mistress had tied it up with a piece of faded red calico and an end of ragged rope. He gave us a civil neigh, and looked at us curiously. Then an impertinent little yellow-and-white dog, with one ear standing up straight and the other drooping over, began to bark with all his might; but he retreated when he saw Kate's great dog, who was walking solemnly by her side and did not deign to notice him. Just now Mrs. Bonny appeared at the door of the house, shading her eyes with her hand, to see who was coming. "Landy!" said she, "if it ain't old Parson Lorimer! And who be these with ye?"

"This is Miss Kate Lancaster of Boston, Miss Katharine Brandon's niece, and her friend Miss Denis."

"Pleased to see ye," said the old woman; "walk in and lay off your things." And we followed her into the house. I wish you could have seen her: she wore a man's coat, cut off so that it made an odd short jacket, and a pair of men's boots much the worse for

Mrs. Bonny's Home

wear; also, some short skirts, beside two or three aprons, the inner one being a full-dress-apron, as she took off the outer ones and threw them into a corner; and on her head was a tight cap, with strings to tie under her chin. I thought it was a nightcap, and that she had forgotten to take it off, and dreaded her mortification if she should suddenly become conscious of it; but I need not have troubled myself, for while we were with her she pulled it on and tied it tighter, as if she considered it ornamental.

There were only two rooms in the house; we went into the kitchen, which was occupied by a flock of hens and one turkey. The latter was evidently undergoing a course of medical treatment behind the stove, and was allowed to stay with us, while the hens were remorselessly hustled out with a hemlock broom. They all congregated on the doorstep, apparently wishing to hear everything that was said.

"B'en up on the mountain?" asked our hostess. "Real sightly place. Goin' to be a master lot o' rosbries; get any down to the shore sence I quit comin'?"

"Oh, yes," said Mr. Lorimer, "but we miss seeing you."

"I s'pose so," said Mrs. Bonny, smoothing her apron complacently; "but I 'm getting old, and I tell 'em I 'm goin' to take my comfort; sence 'he' died I don't put myself out no great; I 've got money enough to keep me long 's I live. Beckett's folks goes down often, and I sends by them for what store stuff I want."

"How are you now?" asked the minister; "I think I heard you were ill in the spring."

"Stirrin', I 'm obliged to ye. I was n't laid up long, and I was so 's I could get about most of the time. I 've got the best bitters ye ever see, good for the spring of the year. S'pose yer sister, Miss Lorimer, would n't like some? she used to be weakly lookin'." But her brother refused the offer, saying that she had not been so well for many years.

"Do you often get out to church nowadays, Mrs. Bonny? I believe Mr. Reid preaches in the school-house sometimes, down by the great ledge; does n't he?"

"Well, yes, he does; but I don't know as I get much of any good. Parson Reid, he 's a worthy creatur', but he never seems to have nothin' to say about foreordination and them p'ints. Old Parson Padelford was the man! I used to set under his preachin' a good deal; I had an aunt living down to East Parish. He 'd get worked up till he 'd shut up the Bible and preach the hair off your head, 'long at the end of the sermon. Could n't understand more nor a quarter part o' what he said," said Mrs. Bonny admiringly. "Well, we were a-speaking about the meeting over to the ledge; I don't know 's I like them ledge people any to speak of. They had a great revival over there in the fall, and one Sunday I thought 's how I 'd go; and when I got there, who should be a-prayin' but old Ben Patey, — he always lays out to get converted, — and he kep' it up diligent till I could n't stand it no longer; and by and by says he, 'I 've been a wanderer;' and I up and says right out, 'Yes, you have, I 'll back ye up on that, Ben; ye 've wandered round my wood-lot and spoilt half the likely young oaks and ashes I 've got, a-stealing your basket-stuff.' And the folks laughed out loud, and up he got and cleared. He 's an awful old thief, and he 's no idea of being anything else. I wa'n't a-goin' to set there and hear him makin' b'lieve to the Lord. If anybody's heart is in it, I ain't a-goin' to hender 'em; I 'm a professor, and I ain't ashamed of it, week-days nor Sundays neither. I can't bear to see folks so pious to meeting, and cheat yer eye-teeth out Monday morning. Well, there! we ain't none of us perfect; even old Parson Moody was round-shouldered, they say."

"You were speaking of the Becketts just now," said Mr. Lorimer (after we had stopped laughing, and Mrs. Bonny had settled her big steel-bowed spectacles and sat looking at him with an expression of extreme wisdom. One might have ventured to call her "peart," I think). "How do they get on? I am seldom in this region nowadays, since Mr. Reid has taken it under his charge."

"They get along somehow or 'nother," replied Mrs. Bonny; "they 've got the best farm this side of the ledge, but they 're dreadful lazy and shiftless, them young folks. Old Mis' Hate-evil Beckett was tellin' me the other day — she that was Samanthy Barnes, you know — that one of the boys got fighting, the other side of the mountain, and come home with his nose broke and a piece o' one ear bit off. I forget which ear it was. Their mother is a real clever, willin' woman, and she takes it to heart, but it 's no use for her to say anything. Mis' Hate-evil Beckett, says she, 'It does make my man feel dreadful to see his brother's folks carry on so.' 'But there,' says I, 'Mis' Beckett, it 's just such things as we read of; Scriptur' is fulfilled: In the larter days there shall be disobedient children.'"

This application of the text was too much for us, but Mrs. Bonny looked serious, and we did not like to laugh. Two or three of the exiled fowls had crept slyly in, dodging underneath our chairs, and had perched themselves behind the stove. They were long-legged, half-grown creatures, and just at this minute one rash young rooster made a manful attempt to crow. "Do tell!" said his mistress, who rose in great wrath; "you need n't be so forth-putting, as I knows on!" After this we were urged to stay and have some supper. Mrs. Bonny assured us she could pick a likely young hen in no time, fry her with a bit of pork, and get us up "a good meat tea;" but we had to disappoint her, as we had some distance to walk to the house where we had left our horses, and a long drive home.

Kate asked if she would be kind enough to lend us a tumbler (for ours was in the basket, which was given into Tommy's charge). We were thirsty, and wished to go back to the spring and get some water.

"Yes, dear," said Mrs. Bonny, "I 've got a glass, if it 's so 's I can find it." And she pulled a chair under the little cupboard over the fireplace, mounted it, and opened the door. Several things fell out at her; and after taking a careful survey she went in, head and shoulders, until I thought that she would disappear altogether; but soon she came back, and reaching in took out one

Mrs. Bonny at Home

treasure after another, putting them on the mantelpiece or dropping them on the floor. There were some bunches of dried herbs, a tin horn, a lump of tallow in a broken plate, a folded newspaper, and an old boot, with a number of turkey-wings tied together, several vials, and a steel trap, and finally, such a tumbler! which she produced with triumph, before stepping down. She poured out of it on the table a mixture of old buttons and squash-seeds, beside a lump of beeswax which she said she had lost, and now pocketed with satisfaction. She wiped the tumbler on her apron and handed it to Kate; but we were not so thirsty as we had been, though we thanked her and went down to the spring, coming back as soon as possible, for we could not lose a bit of the conversation.

There was a beautiful view from the door-step, and we stopped a minute there. "Real sightly, ain't it?" said Mrs. Bonny. "But you ought to be here and look acrost the woods some morning just at sun-up. Why, the sky is all yaller and red, and them low-lands topped with fog! Yes, it's nice weather, good growin' weather, this week. Corn and all the rest of the trade looks first-rate. I call it a forrard season. It's just such weather as we read of, ain't it?"

"I don't remember where, just at this moment," said Mr. Lorimer.

"Why, in the almanac, bless ye!" said she, with a tone of pity in her grum voice; could it be possible he did n't know, — the Deephaven minister!

We asked her to come and see us. She said she had always thought she 'd get a chance some time to see Miss Katharine Brandon's house. She should be pleased to call, and she did n't know but she should be down to the shore before very long. She was 'shamed to look so shif'less that day, but she had some good clothes in a chist in the bedroom, and a boughten bonnet with a good cypress veil, which she had when "he" died. She calculated they would do, though they might be old-fashioned, some. She seemed greatly pleased at Mr. Lorimer's having taken the trouble to come to see her. All those people had a great reverence for "the minister." We were urged to come again in "rosbry" time, which was near at hand, and she gave us messages for some of her old customers and acquaintances. "I believe some of those old creatur's will never die," said she; "why, they 're getting to be ter'ble old, ain't they, Mr. Lorimer? There! ye 've done me a sight of good, and I wish I could ha' found the Bible, to hear ye read a Psalm." When Mr. Lorimer shook hands with her, at leaving, she made him a most reverential courtesy. He was the greatest man she knew; and once during the call, when he was speaking of serious things in his simple, earnest way, she had so devout a look, and seemed so interested, that Kate and I, and Mr. Lorimer himself, caught a new, fresh meaning in the familiar words he spoke.

Living there in the lonely clearing, deep in the woods and far from any neighbor, she knew all the herbs and trees, and the harmless wild creatures who lived among them, by heart; and she had an amazing store of tradition and superstition, which made her so entertaining to us that we went to see her many times before we came away in the autumn. We went with her to find some pitcher-plants one day, and it was wonderful how much she knew about the woods, what keen observation she had. There was something so wild and unconventional about Mrs. Bonny that it was like taking an afternoon walk with a good-natured Indian. We used to carry her offerings of tobacco, for she was a great smoker, and advised us to try it ourselves if ever we should be troubled with nerves, or "narves," as she pronounced the name of that affliction.

In Shadow

SOON after we went to Deephaven we took a long drive one day with Mr. Dockum, the kindest and silentest of men. He had the care of the Brandon property, and had some business at that time connected with a large tract of pasture-land perhaps ten miles from town. We had heard of the coast road which led to it, — how rocky and how rough and wild it was, and when Kate heard by chance that Mr. Dockum meant to go that way, she asked if we might go with him. He said he would much rather take us than "go sole alone," but he should be away until late and we must take our dinner, which we did not mind doing at all.

After we were three or four miles from Deephaven, the country looked very different. The shore was so rocky that there were almost no places where a boat could put in, so there were no fishermen in the region, and the farms were scattered wide apart; the land was so poor that even the trees looked hungry. At the end of our drive we left the horse at a lonely little farmhouse close by the sea. Mr. Dockum was to walk a long way inland through the woods with a man whom he had come to meet, and he told us if we followed the shore westward a mile or two we should find some very high rocks, for which he knew we had a great liking. It was a delightful day to spend out of doors; there was an occasional whiff of salt east-wind. Seeing us seemed to be a perfect godsend to the people whose nearest neighbors lived far out of sight. We had a long talk with them before we went for our walk. The house was close by the water by a narrow cove, around which the rocks were low; but farther down the shore the land rose more and more, and at last we stood at the edge of the highest rocks of all and looked far down at the sea, dashing its white spray high over the ledges that quiet day. What could it be in winter when there was a storm and the great waves came thundering in?

After we had explored the shore to our hearts' content and were tired, we rested for a while in the shadow of some gnarled pitch-pines which stood close together, as near the sea as they dared. They looked like a band of outlaws, they were such wild-looking trees. They seemed very old, and as if their savage fights with the winter winds had made them hard-hearted. And yet the little wild-flowers and the thin green grass-blades were growing fearlessly close around their feet; and there were some comfortable birds'-nests in safe corners of their rough branches.

When we went back to the house at the cove, we had to wait some time for Mr. Dockum. We succeeded in making friends with the children, and gave them some candy and the rest of our lunch, which luckily had been even more abundant than usual. They looked thin and pitiful; but even in that lonely place, where they so seldom saw a stranger or even a neighbor, they showed that there was an evident effort to make them look like other children, and they were neatly dressed, though there could be no mistake about their being very poor. One forlorn little soul, with honest gray eyes and a sweet, shy smile, showed us a string of beads which she wore round her neck ; there were perhaps two dozen of them, blue and white, on a bit of twine, and they were the dearest things in all her world. When we came away we were so glad that we could give the man more than he asked us for taking care of the horse, and his thanks touched us.

"I hope ye may never know what it is to earn every dollar as hard as I have. I never earned any money as easy as this before. I don't feel as if I ought to take it. I 've done the best I could," said the man, with the tears coming into his eyes, and a huskiness in his voice. "I 've done the best I could, and I 'm willin' and my woman is, but everything seems to have been ag'in' us ; we never seem to get forehanded. It looks sometimes as if the Lord had forgot us, but my woman, she never wants me to say that ; she says He ain't, and that we might be worse off, — but I don' know. I have n't had my health ; that 's hendered me most. I 'm a boat-builder by trade, but the business 's all run down ; folks buys 'em second-hand nowadays, and you can't make nothing. I can't stand it to foller deep-sea fishing, and — well, you see what my land 's wuth. But my oldest boy, he 's getting ahead. He pushed off this spring, and he works in a box-shop to Boston; a cousin o' his mother's got him the chance. He sent me ten dollars a spell ago and his mother a shawl. I don't see how he done it, but he 's smart!"

This seemed to be the only bright spot in their lives, and we admired the shawl and sat down in the house awhile with the mother, who seemed kind and patient and tired, and to have great delight in talking about what one should wear. Kate and I thought and spoke often of these people afterward; and when one day we met the man in Deephaven, we sent some things to the children and his wife, and begged him to come to the house whenever he came to town. But we never saw him again; and though we made many plans for going again to the cove, we never did. At one time the road was reported impassable, and we put off our second excursion for this reason and others until just before we left Deephaven, late in October.

We knew the coast-road would be bad after the fall rains, and we found that Leander, the eldest of the Dockum boys, had some errand that way, so he went with us. We enjoyed the drive that morning in spite of the rough road. The air was warm, and sweet with the smell of bayberry-bushes and pitch-pines and the delicious saltness of the sea, which was not far from us all the way. It was a perfect autumn day. Sometimes we crossed pebble beaches, and then went

A Pebble Beach

farther inland, through woods and up and down steep little hills ; over shaky bridges which crossed narrow salt creeks in the marsh-lands. There was a little excitement about the drive, and an exhilaration in the air, and we laughed at jokes forgotten the next minute, and sang, and were jolly enough. Leander, who had never happened to see us in exactly this hilarious state of mind before, seemed surprised and interested, and became unusually talkative, telling us a great many edifying particulars about the people whose houses we passed, and who owned every wood-lot along the road. "Do you see that house over on the p'int?" he asked. "An old fellow lives there that 's part lost his mind. He had a son who was drowned off Cod Rock fishing, much as twenty-five years ago; and he 's worn a deep path out to the end of the p'int, where he goes out every hand's turn o' the day to see if he can't see the boat coming in." And Leander looked round to see if we were not amused, and seemed puzzled because we did n't laugh. Happily, his next story was funny.

We saw a sleepy little owl muffled up on the dead branch of a pine-tree; we saw a rabbit cross the road and disappear in a clump of juniper, and squirrels run up and down trees and along the stone-walls with acorns in their mouths. We passed straggling thickets of the upland sumach, leafless, and holding high their ungainly spikes of red berries; there were sturdy barberry-bushes along the lonely wayside, their unpicked fruit hanging in brilliant clusters. The blueberry-bushes made patches of dull red along the hillsides. The ferns were whitish-gray and brown at the edges of the woods, and the asters and golden-rods which had lately looked so gay in the open fields stood now in faded, frost-bitten companies. There were busy flocks of birds flitting from field to field, ready to start on their journey southward.

When we reached the house, to our surprise there was no one in sight and the place looked deserted. We left the wagon ; and while Leander went toward the barn, which stood at a little distance, Kate and I went to the house and knocked. I opened the door a little way and said " Hello ! " but nobody answered. The people could not have moved away, for there were some chairs standing outside the door, and as I looked in I saw the bunches of herbs hanging up, and a trace of corn, and the furniture was all there. It was a great disappointment, for we had counted upon seeing the children again. Leander said there was nobody at the barn, and that they must have gone to a funeral ; he could n't think of anything else.

Just now we saw some people coming up the road, and we thought at first that they were the man and his wife coming back ; but they proved to be strangers, and we eagerly asked what had become of the family.

"They 're dead, both on 'em. His wife, she died about nine weeks ago last Sunday, and he died day before yesterday. Funeral 's going to be this afternoon. Thought ye were some of her folks from up country, when we were coming along," said the man.

"Guess they won't come nigh," said the woman scornfully; "'fraid they 'd have to help provide for the children. I was half-sister to him, and I 've got to take the two least ones."

"Did you say he was going to be buried this afternoon?" asked Kate slowly. We were both more startled than I can tell.

"Yes," said the man, who seemed much better natured than his wife. She appeared like a person whose only aim in life was to have things over with. "Yes, we 're going to bury at two o'clock. They had a master sight of trouble, first and last."

Leander had said nothing all this time. He had known the man, and had expected to spend the day with him and to get him to go on two miles farther to help bargain for a dory. He asked, in a disappointed way, what had carried him off so sudden.

"Drink," said the woman relentlessly. "He ain't been good for nothing sence his wife died; she was took with a fever along in the first of August. *I* 'd ha' got up from it!"

"Now don't be hard on the dead, Marthy," said her husband. "I guess they done the best they could. They were n't so shif'less, you know; they never had no health: 't was against wind and tide with 'em all the time." And Kate asked, "Did you say he was your brother?"

"Yes. I was half-sister to him," said the woman promptly, with perfect unconsciousness of Kate's meaning.

"And what will become of those poor children?"

"I 've got the two youngest over to my place to take care on, and the two next them has been put out to some folks over to the cove. I dare say like 's not they 'll be sent back."

"They 're clever child'n, I guess," said the man, who spoke as if this were the first time he had dared take their part. "Don't be ha'sh, Marthy! Who knows but they may do for us when we get to be old?" And then she turned and looked at him with utter contempt. "I can't stand it to hear men-folks talking on what they don't know nothing about," said she. "The ways of Providence is dreadful myster'ous," she went on with a whine, instead of the sharp tone of voice which we had heard before. "We 've had a hard row, and we 've just got our own children off our hands and able to do for themselves, and now here are these to be fetched up."

"But perhaps they 'll be a help to you; they seem to be good little things," said Kate. "I saw them in the summer, and they seemed to be pleasant children, and it is dreadfully hard for them to be left alone. It 's not their fault, you know. We brought over something for them; will you be kind enough to take the basket when you go home?"

"Thank ye, I 'm sure," said the aunt, relenting slightly. "You can speak to my man about it, and he 'll give it to somebody that 's going by. I 've got to walk in the procession. They 'll be obliged, I 'm sure. I s'pose you 're the young ladies that come here right after the Fourth o' July, ain't you? I should be pleased to have you call and see the child'n, if you 're over this way again. I heard 'em talk about you last time I was over. Won't ye step into the house and see him? He looks real natural," she added. But we said, "No, thank you."

Leander told us he believed he would n't

bother about the dory that day, and he should be there at the house whenever we were ready. He evidently considered it a piece of good luck that he had happened to arrive in time for the funeral. We spoke to the man about the things we had brought for the children, which seemed to delight him, poor soul, and we felt sure he would be kind to them. His wife shouted to him from a window of the house that he 'd better not loiter round, or they would n't be half ready when the folks began to come, and we said good-by to him and went away.

It was a beautiful morning, and we walked slowly along the shore to the high rocks and the pitch-pine trees which we had seen before; the air was deliciously fresh, and one could take long, deep breaths of it. The tide was coming in, and the spray dashed higher and higher. We climbed about the rocks and went down in some of the deep, cold clefts into which the sun could seldom shine. We gathered some wild-flowers: bits of pimpernel and one or two sprigs of fringed gentian which had bloomed late in a sheltered place, and a pale little bouquet of asters. We sat for a long time looking off to sea, and we could talk or think of almost nothing beside what we had seen and heard at the farmhouse. We said how much we should like to go to the funeral, and we even made up our minds to go back in season, but we gave up the idea: we had no right there, and it would seem as if we were merely curious, and we were afraid our presence would make the people ill at ease, the minister especially. It would be an intrusion.

We spoke of the children, and tried to think what could be done for them: we were afraid they would be told so many times that it was lucky they did not have to go to the poor-house, and yet we could not help pitying the hard-worked, discouraged woman whom we had seen, in spite of her bitterness. Poor soul! she looked like a person to whom nobody had ever been very kind, and for whom life had no pleasures: its sunshine had never been warm enough to thaw the ice at her heart.

We remembered how we knocked at the door and called loudly, but there had been no answer, and we wondered how we should have felt if we had gone farther into the room and had found the dead man in his coffin, all alone in the house. We thought of our first visit, and what he had said to us, and we wished we had come again sooner, for we might have helped them so much more if we had only known.

The Funeral

"What a pitiful ending it is," said Kate. "Do you realize that the family is broken up, and the children are to be half strangers to each other? Did you not notice that they seemed very fond of each other when we saw them in the summer? There was not half the roughness and apparent carelessness of one another which one so often sees in the country. Theirs was such a little world; one can understand how, when the man's wife died, he was bewildered and discouraged, utterly at a loss. The thoughts of winter, and of the little children, and of the struggles he had already come through against poverty and disappointment were terrible thoughts; and like a boat adrift at sea, the waves of his misery brought him in against the rocks, and his simple life was wrecked."

"I suppose his grandest hopes and wishes would have been realized in a good farm and a thousand or two dollars in safe keeping," said I. "Do you remember that merry little song in 'As You Like It'?

> 'Who doth ambition shun
> And loves to live i' the sun,
> Seeking the food he eats,
> And pleased with what he gets;'

and

> 'Here shall he see
> No enemy
> But winter and rough weather.'

That is all he lived for, his literal daily bread. I suppose what would be prosperity to him would be miserably insufficient for some other people. I wonder how we can help being conscious, in the midst of our comforts and pleasures, of the lives which are being starved to death in more ways than one."

"I suppose one thinks more about these things as one grows older," said Kate thoughtfully. "How seldom life in this world seems to be a success! Among rich or poor, only here and there one touches satisfaction, though the one who seems to have made an utter failure may really be the greatest conqueror. And, Helen, I find that I understand better and better how unsatisfactory, how purposeless and disastrous, any life must be which is not a Christian life. It is like being always in the dark, and wandering one knows not where, if one is not learning more and more what it is to have friendship with God."

By the middle of the afternoon the sky had grown cloudy, and a wind seemed to be coming in off the sea, and we unwillingly decided that we must go home. We supposed that the funeral would be all over with, but found we had been mistaken when we reached the cove. We seated ourselves on a rock near the water; just beside us was the old boat, with its killick and painter stretched ashore, where its owner had left it.

There were several men standing around the door of the house, looking solemn and important, and by and by one of them came over to us. We found, too late, that it would have been much better for us to go in, and we learned a little more of the sad story. We liked this man, there was so much pity in his face and voice. "He was a real willin', honest man, Andrew was," said our new friend, "but he used to be sickly, and seemed to have no luck, though for a year or two he got along some better. When his wife died he was sore afflicted, and could n't get over it, and he did n't know what to do or what was going to become of 'em with winter comin' on, and — well — I may 's well tell ye; he took to drink and it killed him right off. I come over two or three times and made some gruel and fixed him up 's well 's I could, and the little gals done the best they could; but he faded right out, and did n't know anything the last time I see him, and he died Sunday mornin', when the tide begun to ebb. I always set a good deal by Andrew; we used to play together down to the great cove;

that's where he was raised, and my folks lived there too. I've got one o' the little gals. I always knowed him and his wife."

Just now we heard the people in the house singing "China," the Deephaven funeral hymn, and the tune suited well that day, with its wailing rise and fall; it was strangely plaintive. Then the funeral exercises were over, and the man with whom we had just been speaking led to the door a horse and rickety wagon, from which the seat had been taken; and when the coffin had been put in, he led the horse down the road a little way, and we watched the mourners come out of the house two by two. We heard some one scold in a whisper because the wagon was twice as far off as it need have been. They evidently had a rigid funeral etiquette, and felt it important that everything should be carried out according to rule. We saw a forlorn-looking kitten, with a bit of faded braid round its neck, run across the road in terror and presently appear again on the stone-wall, where she sat looking at the people. We saw the dead man's eldest son, of whom he had told us in the summer with such pride. He had shown his respect for his father as best he could, by a black band on his hat and a pair of black cotton gloves a world too large for him. He looked so sad, and cried bitterly, as he stood alone at the head of the people. His aunt was next, with a handkerchief at her eyes, fully equal to the proprieties of the occasion, though I fear her grief was not so heartfelt as her husband's, who dried his eyes on his coat-sleeve again and again. There were perhaps twenty of the mourners, and there was much whispering among those who walked last. The minister and some others fell into line, and the procession went slowly down the slope; a strange shadow had fallen over everything. It was like a November day, for the air felt cold and bleak. There were some great sea-fowl high in the air, fighting their way toward the sea against the wind, and giving now and then a wild, far-off ringing cry. We could hear the dull sound of the sea, and at a little distance from the land the waves were leaping high, and breaking in white foam over the isolated ledges.

The rest of the people began to walk or drive away, but Kate and I stood watching the funeral as it crept along the narrow, crooked road. We had never seen what the people called "walking funerals" until we came to Deephaven, and there was something piteous about this; the mourners looked so few, and we could hear the rattle of the wagon wheels. "He 's gone, ain't he?" said some one near us. That was it, —*gone.*

Before the people had entered the house, there had been, I am sure, an indifferent, business-like look; but when they came out, all that was changed: their faces were awed by the presence of death, and the indifference had given place to uncertainty. Their neighbor was immeasurably their superior now. Living, he had been a failure by their own low standards; but now, if he could come back, he would know secrets, and be wise beyond anything they could imagine; and who could know the riches of which he might have come into possession?

To Kate and me there came a sudden consciousness of the mystery and inevitableness of death; it was not fear, thank God! but a thought of how certain it was that some day it would be a mystery to us no longer. And there was a thought, too, of the limitation of this present life; we were waiting there, in company with the people, the great sea, and the rocks and fields themselves, on this side the boundary. We knew just then how close to this familiar, every-day world might be the other, which at times before had seemed so far away, out of reach of even our thoughts, beyond the distant stars.

We stayed awhile longer, until the little black funeral had crawled out of sight; until we had seen the last funeral guest go away and the door had been shut and fastened with a queer old padlock and some

Forsaken

links of rusty chain. The door fitted loosely, and the man gave it a vindictive shake, as if he thought that the poor house had somehow been to blame, and that after a long, desperate struggle for life under its roof and among the stony fields, the family must go away defeated. It is not likely that any one else will ever go to live there. The man to whom the farm was mortgaged will add the few forlorn acres to his pasture-land, and the thistles which the man who is dead had fought so many years will march in next summer and take unmolested possession.

I think to-day of that fireless, empty, forsaken house, where the winter sun shines in and creeps slowly along the floor; the bitter cold is in and around the house, and the snow has sifted in at every crack; outside it is untrodden by any living creature's footstep. The wind blows and rushes and shakes the loose window-sashes in their frames, while the padlock knocks — knocks against the door.

Miss Chauncey

THE Deephaven people used to say sometimes, complacently, that certain things or certain people were "as dull as East Parish." Kate and I grew curious to see that part of the world which was considered duller than Deephaven itself; and as upon inquiry we found that it was not out of reach, one day we went there.

It was like Deephaven, only on a smaller scale. The village — though it is a question whether that is not an exaggerated term to apply — had evidently seen better days. It was on the bank of a river, and perhaps half a mile from the sea. There were a few untouched old buildings there, some with mossy roofs and a great deal of yellow lichen on the sides of the walls next the sea ; a few newer houses, belonging to fishermen; some dilapidated fish-houses; and a row of fish-flakes. Every house seemed to have a lane of its own, and all faced different ways except two fish-houses, which stood amiably side by side. There was a church, which we had been told was the oldest in the region. Through the windows we saw the high pulpit and sounding-board, and finally found the great keys at a house near by; so we went in and looked around at our leisure. A rusty foot-stove stood in one of the old square pews, and in the gallery there lay a majestic bass-viol with all its strings snapped but the largest, which gave out a doleful sound when we touched it, and somehow looked very uncomfortable until we built up a pillow of hymn books under its head.

After we left the church we walked along the road a little way, and came in sight of a fine old house which had apparently fallen into ruin years before. The front entrance was a fine specimen of old-fashioned workmanship, with its columns and carvings, and the fence had been a grand affair in its day, though now it could scarcely stand alone. The long range of out-buildings was falling piece by piece; one shed had been blown down entirely by a late high wind. The large windows had many small panes of glass, and the great chimneys were built of bright red bricks which used to be brought from overseas in the early days of the colonies. We noticed the gnarled lilacs in the yard, the wrinkled cinnamon-roses, and a flourishing company of French pinks, or "bouncing Bets," as Kate called them.

"Suppose we go in," said I ; "the door is open a little way. There surely must be some stories about its being haunted. We can ask Miss Honora." And we climbed over the boards which were put up like pasture-bars across the wide front gateway.

"We shall certainly meet a ghost," said Kate.

Just as we stood on the steps the great door was pulled wide open ; we started back, and, well-grown young women as we are, we have confessed since that our first impulse was to run away. On the threshold there stood a stately old woman who looked surprised at first sight of us, then quickly recovered herself and stood waiting for us to speak. She was dressed in a rusty black satin gown, with scant, short skirt and huge sleeves; on her head was a great black bonnet with a high crown and a close brim, which came far out over her face.

"What is your pleasure?" said she; and we felt like two awkward children. Kate partially recovered her wits, and asked which was the nearer way to Deephaven.

"There is but one road, past the church and over the hill. It cannot be missed." And she bowed gravely, when we thanked her and begged her pardon, we hardly knew why, and came away.

We looked back to see her still standing in the doorway. "Who in the world can she be?" said Kate, but we wondered and puzzled and talked over "the ghost" until we saw Miss Honora Carew, who told us that it was Miss Sally Chauncey.

"Indeed, I know her, poor old soul!" said Miss Honora. "She has such a sad history. She is the last survivor of one of the most aristocratic old colonial families. The Chaunceys were people of great renown until early in the present century, and then their fortunes changed. They had always been rich and well educated; and I suppose nobody ever had a gayer, happier time than Miss Sally did in her girlhood, for they entertained a great deal of company and lived in fine style. But her father was unfortunate in business, and at last was utterly ruined at the time of the embargo; then he became

Miss Sally Chauncey

partially insane, and died after many years of poverty. I have often heard a tradition that a sailor had cursed him, to whom he had broken a promise, and that none of the family had died in their beds or had any good fortune since. The East Parish people seem to believe in it, and it is certainly strange what terrible sorrow has come to the Chaunceys. One of Miss Sally's brothers, a fine young officer in the navy, who was at home on leave, asked her one day if she could get on without him, and she said Yes, thinking that he had his orders to go to sea ; but in a few minutes she heard the noise of a pistol in his room, and hurried in to find him lying dead on the floor. Then there was another brother who was insane, and who became so violent that he was chained for years in one of the upper chambers, a dangerous prisoner. I have heard his horrid shrieks myself, when I was a young girl," said Miss Honora, with a shiver.

"Miss Sally is insane, and has been for many years, and this seems to me the saddest part of the story. When she first lost her reason she was sent to a hospital, for there was no one who could take care of her. The mania was so acute that no one had the slightest thought that she would recover or even live long. Her guardian sold the furniture and pictures and china, almost everything but clothing, to pay the bills at the hospital, until the house was fairly empty; and then one spring day — I remember it well — she came home in her right mind, and, without a thought of what was awaiting her, ran eagerly into her destroyed home. It was a terrible shock, and she never has recovered from it, though after a long illness her insanity took a mild form, and she has always been perfectly harmless. She has been alone many years, and no one can persuade her to leave the old house, where she seems to be contented, and does not realize her troubles; though she lives mostly in the past, and has little idea of the present, except in her house affairs, which seem pitiful to me, for I remember the grand housekeeping of the Chaunceys when I was a child. I have been to see her, and she always knows me, though I go but seldom of late years. She is several years older than I. She has some old friends who take care that she does not suffer, though her wants are few. She is an elegant woman still; and some day, if you like, I will give you something to carry to her, and a message, if I can think of one, and you must go to pay her a visit. I hope she will happen to be talkative, for I am sure you would enjoy her. For many years she did not like to see strangers, but some one has told me lately that she seems to be pleased if people go to see her."

You may be sure it was not many days before Kate and I claimed the basket and the message, and went again to East Parish. We boldly lifted the great brass knocker, and were dismayed because nobody answered. While we waited, a girl came up the walk and said that Miss Sally lived upstairs, and she would speak to her if we liked. "Sometimes she don't have sense enough to know what the knocker means," we were told. There was evidently no romance about Miss Sally to our new acquaintance.

"Do you think," said I, "that we might go in? Perhaps she will refuse to see us."

"Yes, indeed," said the girl; "everybody goes right in; she is a little deaf. I'll go and find her, somewhere upstairs."

So we went into the great hall, with its wide staircase and handsome cornices and paneling, and then into the large parlor on the right, and could look through it to a smaller room opening on the garden, which sloped down to the river. Both rooms had fine carved mantels, with Dutch-tiled fireplaces, and in the cornices we saw the fastenings where pictures had hung, — old portraits, perhaps. And what had become of them? The girl did not know: the house had been the same ever since she could remember, only it would all fall through into the cellar soon. But the old lady was proud as Lucifer, and would n't hear of moving out.

The floor in the room toward the river was so broken that it was not safe, and our guide went back through the hall and opened the door at the foot of the stairs. "Guess you won't want to stop long there," said the girl. Three old hens and a rooster marched toward her with great solemnity as she glanced in. The cobwebs hung in the room, as they often do in old barns, in long, gray festoons; the lilacs outside grew close against the two windows where the shutters were not drawn, and the light in the room was greenish and dim.

Kate and I waited while the young neighbor went upstairs and announced us to Miss Sally, and in a few minutes we heard her come along the hall.

"Sophia," said she, "where are the gentry waiting?" And just then she came in sight round the turn of the staircase. She wore the same great black bonnet and satin gown, and looked more old-fashioned and ghostly than before. She was not tall, but very erect, in spite of her great age, and her eyes seemed to "look through you" in an uncanny way. She slowly descended the stairs and came toward us with a courteous greeting; and when we had introduced ourselves as Miss Carew's friends, she gave us each her hand in a most cordial way, and said she was pleased to see us. She bowed us into the parlor and waved us toward two rickety, straight-backed chairs, which, with an old table, were all the furniture there was in the room. "Sit ye down," said she, herself taking a place in the window-seat. I have seen few such elegant women as Miss Chauncey. Thoroughly at her ease, she had the fine manners of a lady of the olden times, using the quaint fashion of speech which she had been taught in her girlhood. The long words and ceremonious phrases suited her extremely well. Her hands were delicately shaped, and she folded them in her lap, as no doubt she had learned to do at boarding-school so many years before. She asked Kate and me if we knew any young ladies at that school in Boston, saying that most of her intimate friends had left when she did, but some of the younger ones were there still.

She asked for the Carews and Mr. Lorimer; and when Kate told her that she was Miss Brandon's niece, and asked if she had not known her, she said, "Certainly, my dear; we were intimate friends at one time, but I have seen her little of late."

"Do you not know that she is dead?" asked Kate.

"Ah, they say that about every one nowadays. I do not comprehend the strange idea!" said the old lady impatiently. "It is an excuse, I suppose. She could come to see me if she chose, but she was always a ceremonious body, and I go abroad but seldom now; so perhaps she waits my visit. I will not speak uncourteously, and you must remember me to her kindly."

Then she asked us about other old people in Deephaven, and about families in Boston whom she had known in her early days. I think every one of whom she spoke was dead, but we assured her that they were all well and prosperous, and believed that we told the truth. She asked about the love-affairs of men and women who had died old and gray-headed within our remembrance; and finally she said we must pardon her for these tiresome questions, but it was so rarely that she saw any one direct from Boston, of whom she could inquire concerning these old friends and relatives of her family.

Something happened after this which touched us both inexpressibly: she sat for some time watching Kate with a bewildered look, which at last faded away, a smile coming in its place. "I think you are like my mother," she said; "did any one ever say to you that you are like my mother? Will you let me see your forehead? Yes; but your hair is a little darker." Kate had risen when Miss Chauncey did, and they stood side by side. There was a tone in the old woman's voice which brought the tears to my eyes. She stood there some minutes looking at Kate, and completely lost in thought. There was a kinship, it seemed to me, not of blood, only that they both were of the same stamp and rank: Miss Chauncey of the old generation and Kate Lancaster of the new. Miss Chauncey turned to me, saying, "Look up at the portrait; you must see the likeness too." But when she turned and saw only the bare wainscoting of the room, she looked puzzled, and the bright flash which had lighted up her face was gone in an instant, and she sat down again in the window-seat; but we were glad that she had forgotten. Presently she said anxiously, "Pardon me, dear, but I forget your question."

Miss Carew had told us to ask her about her school-days, as she nearly always spoke of that time to her; and to our delight, Miss Sally told us a charming long story about her friends and about her "coming-out party," when boat-loads of gay young guests came down from Riverport, and all the gentry from Deephaven. The band from the fort played for the dancing, the garden was lighted, the card-tables were in this room, and a grand supper was served beyond. She even remembered what some of her friends wore, and her own gown was a silver-gray brocade with rosebuds of three colors. She told us how she watched the boats go off up river in the middle of the summer night; how sweet the music sounded; how bright the moonlight was; how she wished we had been there at her party.

"I can't believe I am an old woman. It seems only yesterday," said she thoughtfully. And then she lost the idea, and talked about Kate's great-grandmother, whom she had known well, and asked us how she had been this summer.

She asked us if we would like to go up stairs, where she had a fire, and we eagerly accepted, though we were not in the least cold. Ah, what a sorry place it was! She had gathered together some few pieces of her old furniture, which half filled one fine room, and here she lived. There was a tall, handsome chest of drawers, which I should have liked much to ransack. Miss Carew had told us that Miss Chauncey had large claims against the government, dating back sixty or seventy years, but nobody could ever find the papers; and I felt sure that they must be hidden away in some secret drawer. The brass handles and trimmings were blackened, and the wood looked like ebony. I wished to climb up and look into the upper part of this antique piece of furniture, for it seemed to me I could at once put my hand on a package of "papers relating to the embargo."

On a stand near the window was an old Bible, fairly worn out with constant use. Miss Chauncey was most religious; in fact, it was the only subject about which she was perfectly sane. We saw almost nothing of her insanity that day; it was more like forgetfulness, though afterward she was different. There were days when her mind seemed clear; but sometimes she was silent, and often she would confuse Kate with Miss Brandon, and talk to her strangely of long-forgotten plans and people. She would rarely speak of anything more than a minute or two, and then would drift into an entirely foreign subject.

She urged us that afternoon to stay to luncheon with her; she said she could not offer us dinner, but she would give us tea and biscuit, and no doubt we should find something in Miss Carew's basket, as she was always kind in remembering her fancies. Miss Honora had told us to decline if she asked us to stay; but I should have liked to see her sit at the head of her table, and to be a guest at such a lunch-party.

Poor creature! It was a blessed thing that her shattered reason made her unconscious of the change in her fortunes, and incapable of comparing the end of her life with its beginning. To herself she was still Miss Chauncey, a gentlewoman of high family, possessed of unusual worldly advantages. The remembrance of her cruel trials and sorrows had faded from her mind. She had no idea of the poverty of her surroundings when she paced back and forth, with stately steps, on the ruined terraces of her garden; the ranks of lilies and the conserve-roses were still in bloom for her, and the box-borders were as trimly kept as ever; and when she pointed out to us the distant

Miss Chauncey's Garden

steeples of Riverport, it was plain to see that it was still the Riverport of her girlhood. If the boat-landing at the foot of the garden had long ago dropped into the river and gone out with the tide; if the maids and men who used to do her bidding were all out of hearing; if there had been no dinner company that day and no guests were expected for the evening, — what did it matter? The twilight had closed around her gradually, and she was alone in her house, but she did not heed the ruin of it or the absence of her friends. On the morrow, life would again go on.

We always used to ask her to read the Bible to us, after Mr. Lorimer had told us how touching and beautiful it was to listen to her. I shall never hear some of the Psalms or some chapters of Isaiah again without being reminded of her; and I remember just now, as I write, one summer afternoon when Kate and I had lingered later than usual, and we sat in the upper room looking out on the river and the shore beyond, where the light had begun to grow golden as the day drew near sunset. Miss Chauncey had opened the great book at random and read slowly, "In my Father's house are many mansions;" and then, looking off for a moment at a fallen leaf which had blown into the window-recess, she repeated it: "In my Father's house are many mansions; if it were not so, I would have told you." Then she went on slowly to the end of the chapter, and with her hands clasped together on the Bible she fell into a reverie, and the tears came into our eyes as we watched her look of perfect content. Through all her clouded years the promises of God had been her only certainty.

Miss Chauncey died early in the winter after we left Deephaven, and one day when I was visiting Kate in Boston, Mr. Lorimer came to see us, and told us about her last days.

It seems that after much persuasion she was induced to go to spend the winter with a neighbor, her house having become uninhabitable, and she was, beside, too feeble to live alone. But her fondness for her old home was too strong, and one day she stole away from the people who took care of her, and crept in through the cellar, where she had to go through half-frozen water, and then went upstairs, where she seated herself at a front window and called joyfully to the people who went by, asking them to come in to see her, for now she had got home again.

After this she was very ill; and one day, when she was half delirious, they missed her, and found her at last sitting on her hall stairway, which she was too feeble to climb. She lived but a short time afterwards, and in her last hours her mind seemed perfectly clear. She said over and over again how good God had always been to her, and she was gentle, and unwilling to be a trouble to those who had the care of her.

Mr. Lorimer spoke of her simple goodness, and told us that though she had no other sense of time, and hardly knew if it were summer or winter, she was always sure when Sunday came, and always came to church when he preached at East Parish, her greatest pleasure seeming to be to give money, if there was a contribution. "She may be a lesson to us," added the old minister reverently; "for though bewildered in mind, bereft of friends and riches, and all that makes this world dear to many of us, she was still steadfast in her simple faith, and was never heard to complain of any of the burdens which God had given her."

Last Days in Deephaven

WHEN the summer was ended it was no sorrow to us, for we were even more fond of Deephaven in the glorious autumn weather than we had ever been before. Mr. Lancaster, Kate's father, was abroad longer than he had intended to be at first, and it was late in the season before we left. We were both ready to postpone going back to town as late as possible ; but at last it was time for my friend to reëstablish the Boston housekeeping, and to take up her city life again. I must admit we half dreaded that: we were surprised to find how little we cared for it, and how well one can get on without many things which are thought indispensable.

For the last fortnight we were in the house a good deal, because the weather was wet and dreary. At one time there was a magnificent storm, and we went every day along the shore in the wind and rain for a mile or two to see the furious great breakers come plunging in against the rocks. I never had seen such a wild, stormy sea as that; the rage of it was awful, and the whole harbor was white with foam. The wind had blown northeast steadily for days, and it seemed to me that the sea never could be quiet and smooth and blue again, with soft white clouds sailing over it in the sky. It was a treacherous sea; it was wicked; it had all the trembling land in its power, if it only dared to send the great waves far ashore. All night long the breakers roared, and the wind howled in the chimneys, and in the morning we always looked fearfully across the surf and the tossing gray water to see if the lighthouse were standing firm on its rock. It was so slender a thing to hold its own in such a wide and monstrous sea. But the sun came out at last, and not many days afterward we went out with Danny and Skipper Scudder to say good-by to Mrs. Kew.

I have been many voyages at sea, but I never was so danced about in a little boat as I was that day. There was nothing to fear with so careful a crew, and we only enjoyed the roughness as we went out and in, though it took much manœuvring to land us at the island.

It was very sad work to us — saying good-by to our friends, and we tried to make believe that we should spend the next summer in Deephaven, and we promised at any rate to go down for a visit. We were glad when the people said they should miss us, and that they hoped we should not forget them and the old place. It touched us to find that they cared so much for us; we thought it was only ourselves who had cared so much for them, and we said over and over again how happy we had been, and that it was such a happy summer. Kate laughingly proposed one evening, as we sat talking by the fire and were particularly contented, that we should copy the Ladies of Llangollen, and remove ourselves from society and its distractions.

"I have thought often, lately," said my friend, "what a good time they must have had, and I feel a sympathy and friendliness for them which I never felt before. We could have guests when we chose, as we have had this summer, and we could study and grow very wise; and what could be pleasanter? But I wonder if we should grow very lazy if we stayed here all the year round; village life is not stimulating, and there would not be much to do in winter, though I do not believe that need be true; one may be busy and useful in any place."

"I suppose if we really belonged in Deephaven we should think it a hard fate, and not enjoy it half so much as we have this summer," said I. "Our idea of happiness would be making long visits in Boston; and we should be heart-broken when we had to come away and leave our luncheon-parties, and symphony concerts, and visits, and fairs, the reading-club, and the children's hospital. We should think the people uncongenial and behind the times, and that the Ridge road was stupid and the long sands desolate; while we remembered what delightful walks we had taken out Beacon Street to the three roads, and over the Cambridge Bridge. Perhaps we should even be ashamed of the dear old church for being so out of fashion. We should have the blues dreadfully, and think there was no society here, and wonder why we had to live in such a town."

"What a gloomy picture!" said Kate

laughing. "Do you know that I have understood something lately better than I ever did before? it is that success and happiness are not things of chance with us, but of choice. I can see now how we might easily have had a dull summer here. Of course it is our own fault if the events of our lives are hindrances; it is we who make them bad or good. Sometimes it is a conscious choice, but oftener unconscious. I suppose we educate ourselves for taking the best of life or the worst, do not you?"

"Dear old Deephaven!" said Kate gently, after we had been silent a little while. "It makes me think of one of its own old ladies, with her clinging to the old fashions and her respect for what used to be respectable when she was young. I cannot make fun of what was once dear to somebody, and embodied somebody's ideas of beauty or fitness. I don't dispute the usefulness of a new bustling, manufacturing town with its progressive ideas; but there is a simple dignity in a town like Deephaven, as if it tried to be loyal to the traditions of its ancestors. It quietly accepts its altered circumstances, if it has seen better days, and has no harsh feelings toward the cities which have drawn away its business, but it lives on, making all the old houses and boats and clothes last as long as possible."

"I think one cannot help," said I, "having a different affection for an old place like Deephaven from that which one may have for a newer town. Here, though there are no exciting historical associations and none of the veneration which one has for the very old cities and towns abroad, it is impossible not to remember how many people have walked the streets and lived in the houses. I was thinking to-day how many girls must have grown up in this house, and that their places have been ours; we have inherited their pleasures, and perhaps have carried on work which they began. We sit in somebody's favorite chair and look out of the window at the sea, and dream about our wishes and our hopes and plans just as they did before us. Something of them still lingers where their lives were spent. We are often reminded of our friends who have died and feel their dear presence; why are we not reminded as surely of strangers in such a house as this, — finding some trace of the lives which were lived among the sights we see and the things we handle, as the incense of many masses lingers in some old cathedral, and one catches the spirit of longing and prayer where so many heavy hearts have brought their burdens and have gone away comforted?"

"When I first came here," said Kate, "it used to seem very sad to me to find Aunt

Somebody's Favorite Chair

Katharine's little trinkets and possessions lying about the house. I have often thought of what you have just said. I heard Mrs. Patton say the other day that there is no pocket in a shroud, and of course it is better that we should carry nothing out of this world. Yet I can't help wishing that it were possible to keep some of my worldly goods always. There are one or two books of mine and some little things which I have had a long time, and of which I have grown very fond. It makes me so sorry to think of their being neglected and lost. I cannot believe I shall forget these earthly treasures when I am in heaven, and I wonder if I shall not miss them. Is n't it strange to think of not reading one's Bible any more? I suppose this is a very low view of heaven, don't you?" And we both smiled.

"I think the next dwellers in this house ought to find a decided atmosphere of contentment," said I. "Have you ever thought that it took us some time to make it your house instead of Miss Brandon's? It used to seem to me that it was still under her management, that she was its mistress; but now it belongs to you, and if I were ever to come back without you, I should find you here."

It is bewildering to know that this is the last chapter, and that it must not be long. I remember so many of our pleasures of which I have hardly said a word. There were our guests, of whom I have told you nothing, and of whom there was so much to say. Of course we asked my Aunt Mary to stay with us, and Miss Margaret Tennant, and many of our girl-friends. All our acquaintances who have yachts made the port of Deephaven if they were cruising in the neighboring waters. Once a most cheerful party of Kate's cousins and some other young people whom we knew very well came to visit us in this way, and the yacht was kept in the harbor a week or more, while we were all as gay as bobolinks and went frisking about the country, and kept late hours in the sober old Brandon house. My Aunt Mary, who was with us, and Kate's aunt, Mrs. Thorniford, who knew the Carews, and was commander of the yacht-party, tried to keep us in order, and to make us ornaments to Deephaven society instead of reproaches and stumbling-blocks. Kate's younger brothers were with us, waiting until it was time for them to go back to college, and I think there never had been such picnics in Deephaven before, and I fear there never will be again.

We are fond of reading, and we meant to do a great deal of it, as every one does who goes away for the summer; but I must confess that our grand plans were not well carried out. Our Latin dictionaries were on the table in the west parlor until the sight of them mortified us; and finally, to avoid their silent reproach, I put them in the closet, with the excuse that it would be as easy to find them there, and they would be out of the way. We used to have the magazines sent us from town; you would have smiled at the box of foreign books which we carried to Deephaven, and indeed we sent two or three times for others; but I do not remember that we ever carried out that course of study which we had planned with so much interest. We were out of doors so much that there was often little time for anything else.

Kate said one day that she did not care, in reading, to be always making new acquaintances, but to be seeing more of old ones; and I think it a very wise idea. We each have our pet books; Kate carries with her a much-worn copy of "Mr. Rutherford's Children," which has been her delight ever since she can remember. Sibyl and Chryssa are dear old friends, though I suppose now it is not merely what Kate reads, but what she associates with the story. I am not often separated from Jean Ingelow's "Stories told to a Child," that charmingly wise and pleasant little volume. It is always new, like Kate's favorite. It is very hard to make a list of the books one likes best, but I remember that we had "The Village on the Cliff," and "Henry Esmond," and "Tom Brown at Rugby," with his more serious ancestor, "Sir Thomas Browne." I am sure we had "Fénelon's Letters and Sermons," for we always have those wherever we are; and there was "Pet Marjorie," and "Rab," and "Annals of a Parish," and "The Life of the Reverend Sydney Smith;" beside Miss Tytler's "Days of Yore," and "The Holy and Profane State," by Thomas Fuller, from which Kate gets so much entertainment and profit. We did read some of Mr. Emerson's essays together, out of doors, and several plays of Shakespeare and some stories which had been our dear friends at school, like "Leslie Goldthwaite," for old time's sake. There was a very good library in the house, and we both like old books, so we enjoyed that. And we used to read the Spectator, and many old-fashioned stories and essays and sermons, with much more pleasure because they had such quaint old brown leather bindings. You will not doubt that we had brought all our most cherished volumes of poetry, or that we used to read them aloud to each other when we sat in our favorite corner of the rocks at the shore, or were in the pine woods of an afternoon.

We used to go out to take tea, and to dine and do a great deal of social visiting, which was very pleasant. It was a great attention to be asked to spend the day, which courtesy we used to delight in extending to our friends; and we entertained in that way often. When we first went out, we were somewhat interesting on account of our clothes, which were of later pattern than had been adopted generally in Deephaven. We used to take great pleasure in arraying ourselves on high days and holidays, since when we went wandering on shore, or out sailing or rowing, we did not always dress as befitted our position in the town: fish-scales and blackberry-briers so soon disfigure one's every-day clothes.

We became in the course of time learned in all manner of 'longshore lore, and even profitably employed ourselves one morning in going clam-digging with old Ben Horn, a most fascinating ancient mariner. We both grew perfectly well and brown and strong, and Kate and I did not get tired of each other at all, which I think was wonderful, for few friendships would bear such a test. We were together always, and alone together a great deal, and we became wonderfully well acquainted. We are such good friends that we often were silent for a long time, when mere acquaintances would have felt compelled to talk and try to entertain each other.

Before we left, the leaves had fallen off all the trees except the oaks, which make in cold weather one of the dreariest sounds one ever hears: a shivering rustle, which makes one pity the tree and imagine it shelterless and forlorn. The sea had looked rough and cold for many days, and the old house itself had grown chilly, — all the world seemed waiting for the snow to come. There was nobody loitering on the wharves, and when we went down the street we walked fast, arm in arm, to keep warm. The houses were shut up as close as possible, and the old sailors did not seem cheery any longer; they looked forlorn, and it was not a pleasant prospect to be so long weather-bound in port. If they ventured out, they put on ancient great-coats, with huge flaps to the pockets and large horn buttons, and they looked contemptuously at the vane, which always pointed to the north or east. It felt like winter, and the captains rolled more than ever as they walked, as if they were on deck in a heavy sea. The rheumatism claimed many victims; and there was one day, it must be confessed, when a biting,

Clam Digging

icy fog was blown in-shore, that Kate and I were willing to admit that we could be as comfortable in town, and it was almost time for sealskin jackets.

In the front yards we saw the flower-beds black with frost, except a few brave pansies which had kept green and bloomed under the tall china-aster stalks, and one day we picked some of these little flowers to put between the leaves of a book and take away with us. I think we loved Deephaven all the more in those last days, with a bit of compassion in our tenderness for the dear old town, which had so little to amuse it. So long a winter was coming; but we thought with a sigh, how pleasant it would be in the spring.

You would have smiled at the treasures we brought away with us; we had become so fond of even our fishing-lines; and this very day you may see in Kate's room two great bunches of Deephaven cat-o'-nine-tails. They were much in our way on the journey home, but we clung affectionately to these last sheaves of our harvest.

The morning we came away our friends were all looking out from door or window to see us go by; and after we had passed the last house and there was no need to smile any longer, we were very dismal. The sun was shining again bright and warm, as if the Indian summer were beginning, and we wished that it had been a rainy day.

The thought of Deephaven will always bring to us our long, quiet summer days, and reading aloud on the rocks by the sea, the fresh salt air, and the glory of the sunsets ; the wail of the Sunday psalm-singing at church, the yellow lichen that grew over the trees, the houses, and the stone-walls; our boating and wanderings ashore; our unlooked-for importance as members of society, and how kind every one was to us both. By and by the Deephaven warehouses will fall and be used for firewood by the fisher-people, and the wharves will be worn away by the tides. The few old gentlefolks who still linger will be dead then; and I wonder if some day Kate Lancaster and I may not go down to Deephaven for the sake of old times, and read the epitaphs in the burying-ground, look out to sea, and talk quietly about the two girls who were so happy there one summer long before. I should like to walk along the beach at sunset, and watch the color of the marshes and the sea change as the light of the sky goes out. It would make the old days come back vividly. We should see the roofs and chimneys of the village, and the great Chantrey elms look black against the sky. A little later the marsh fog would show faintly white, and we should feel it deliciously cold and wet against our hands and faces; when we looked up there would be a star; the crickets would chirp loudly; perhaps some late sea-birds would fly inland. Turning, we should see the lighthouse lamp shine out over the water, and the great sea would move and speak to us lazily in its idle, high-tide sleep.